*A
Harlequin
Romance*

OTHER
Harlequin Romances
by VIOLET WINSPEAR

RAINTREE VALLEY

by

VIOLET WINSPEAR

HARLEQUIN BOOKS

TORONTO   •   WINNIPEG

Orginal hard cover edition published in 1971
by Mills & Boon Limited, 17-19 Foley Street,
London W1A 1DR, England.

© Violet Winspear 1971

Harlequin edition published January, 1972

SBN 373-01555-0

Reprinted May, 1972

Printed in Canada

CHAPTER ONE

THE long-distance bus had passed through country almost tropical and skirted the long rustling waves of sugar-cane. Now the air smelt of the sea, for they had crossed the border and were travelling along the coastline of Brisbane.

Joanna gazed from the window of the bus and hoped that the job she was bound for would be as interesting as the name of the place where it awaited her. Raintree Valley had a romantic sound to it, but she might again be disappointed at her journey's end. She drew a sigh, and a glance from the person sitting beside her. A glance that took in her ash-blonde hair, blue suit, and slender, ringless hands. To all outward appearances Joanna Dowling had a cool, composed, almost reserved air, but inwardly she was taut with nerves.

She had come to this faraway country to live with her sister Viviana, and she hadn't dreamed that her twin was still as impulsive and irresponsible as she had been at sixteen, when she had packed a suitcase and run off to London to go on the stage.

Gay, attractive, self-seeking Viviana, just an hour younger than Joanna but different in every way. She had disliked everything at school except the dancing lessons, and living on a farm with a rather stern grandmother had never been her idea of fun. She had cut loose and wheedled her way into chorus work, and when the show had travelled to Australia she had stayed there and found stage work in Sydney. Then out of the blue she had written to suggest that Joanna join her.

'There are no more drawbacks, Jo,' she had written in her persuasive way. 'You've done your duty by Gran and now she's giving up the farm and settling in with her sister, you're free to live your own life. Come to Australia, pet! We'll be together again, as twins should be, not miles apart.'

Gran had been against the idea when Joanna had broached it. 'You mark my words, girl,' she said. 'You'll get there and then Viv'll leave you flat to go gallivanting off somewhere else. She's as footloose as your father was. He dragged your poor mother all over the globe, planting one thing and another without ever planting himself and his family in a proper home. Viv takes after him! She's every bit as charming and selfish. You mark what I say, Jo. She'll charm you into going out to her, and then she'll leave you stranded!'

Well, it had happened, just as Gran had predicted.

Joanna's journey had ended in twins not meeting, and the manager of the theatre had been left with the task of telling her that Viviana had gone off to New Zealand to star in a musical show. It was her first really big break. A chance she couldn't miss. She left heaps of loving apologies, but was sure Joanna would make out fine in Australia, where she could make a life of her own without being tied to Gran's apron strings.

No, it did no good to weep over Viviana, but Joanna had felt very much stranded for a week or two. The lease on her sister's apartment had run out, so she booked in at a small, inexpensive hotel, and it was there in the potted lounge that a sun-lined outback widow had suggested that she try for a job on one of the sheep or cattle stations where girls used to farm work were always in demand.

Joanna scanned the situation columns in the various newspapers and her eye was caught and held by one job

6

in particular. Her heart beat fast as she read the requirements of the situation. It was on a cattle station, where a young and active woman was needed to help in the home and to provide companionship for a young person. The homestead was situated in a place called Raintree Valley.

Unlike her sister, Joanna had never been fond of bright city lights and though she could have found work as a waitress or a receptionist in a Sydney hotel, she had a love of the country and Raintree Valley sounded just her sort of place. She replied to the box number of the advertisement and asked the outback widow if she had ever heard of the valley. Australia was a mighty big place, the woman reminded her. It could be way up in Queensland.

Several days passed and to fill in time Joanna went to the zoo to look at the animals she would probably meet in the Australian wilds. She loved the furry koala bears and the big kangaroos that looked so odd and friendly; the birds of paradise amazed her with their dazzling plumage. She sent off a coloured postcard to her grandmother, assuring her that all was well and that she hoped to land a job in the very near future.

She was more hopeful than optimistic, for these people at Raintree Valley might prefer to employ an Australian girl rather than one who was fresh out from England and green to the ways of the graziers.

Then to her delight she received a reply to her application. It was written in beautiful longhand on good quality notepaper, in a style that had gone out at the turn of the century, and was signed very regally with the name Charlotte Maud Corraine, Miss.

Miss Dowling's qualifications for the post met with Miss Corraine's approval, and that she was English was also most satisfactory. She would be required to take the long-distance coach from Sydney to Brisbane, where she would alight at Hawk's Bay to be met by a member of the Corraine ménage, who would escort her the remainder of the way to Raintree Valley. There was a small hotel at Hawk's Bay known as the Spearfish and there Miss Dowling would be met by Mr. Vance Corraine.

Joanna was charmed by the letter and only too eager to obey its instructions, and now here on the bus she and several other passengers were gathering their hand luggage together in readiness for the arrival at Hawk's Bay. Joanna took out her compact and powdered her nose. Her eyes were eager and as always her hair was smooth in its chignon. She pulled on her gloves and saw palm trees waving along a pale sandy beach as the bus slowed down and there was a hiss of hydraulic brakes and a sliding open of the doors.

Because of the old-world charm of Miss Corraine's letter, Joanna had half expected Hawk's Bay to be old-fashioned. On the contrary! There were ice-cream parlours and boutiques along the seafront, and young men and girls were gaily surfing out on the rolling blue water. And the smell of steak and onions hung on the sea air as she alighted from the bus and there was a brightly painted air about the place that slightly disappointed her. Her romantic imagination had built a picture of the bay as it must have looked a long time ago, when Charlotte Corraine had been a girl. How long had it been since Miss Corraine had left the valley if she still wrote about this place as if it were untouched by tourism?

The Spearfish Hotel was as modern as the sun-tanned girls in their gay beachwear; sparkling with glass and polish, and with a cocktail bar leading off the lounge.

Joanna inquired at the desk for Vance Corraine and

8

was informed that Mr. Corraine had gone out surfing and would meet her in the cocktail bar at six o'clock. She could if she wished use his suite to freshen up after her long trip.

'Oh – thank you.' Joanna accepted the key with a slight feeling of trepidation. There was something about the name Vance, and the fact that the man liked surfing, that conjured up a lean, alert and self-confident figure. But she did feel rather warm and creased and it would be nice to take a shower and to change into a dress. . . .

'I might as well book a room,' she began.

The clerk shook his head. 'We're full right up, miss. Besides I understood that Mr. Corraine would be checking out right after he dines here tonight. You'll be going with him, won't you? He came in his plane and will be flying home.'

'His plane?' she echoed, feeling more than ever that she had become involved with people who were not simple, down-to-earth farmers.

The clerk smiled a little, aware from her accent that she was from England, and from the bewilderment in her smoke-blue eyes that she was a stranger to the man she was to meet here. She glanced at the key in her hand. 'Did Mr. Corraine say when he would be in?' she asked a trifle nervously.

'When an Australian gets into the water, miss . . .' The clerk shrugged significantly. 'Maybe around sundown.'

'Of course.' Joanna felt a little thrill of wonderment run through her. Vance Corraine was an Australian and she would be working for his family. Strangely enough, no doubt because of Charlotte Corraine's letter, she had been thinking of these people as almost English.

A bellboy carried her suitcase to the lift and she was whisked up to a suite that was obviously one of the best at the hotel. She took a cool shower – still feeling nervous in case some brawny six-footer suddenly appeared – and changed into a sleeveless dress with a softly pleated skirt. The Australian sun slanted through the wide windows of the room and the sea-light danced on the ceiling, and she noticed as she tidied her hair in front of the dressing-table mirror that she looked rather pale. She pinched her cheeks and wondered how Viviana was making out in New Zealand.

Happy-go-lucky Viv, who never worried about tomorrow as Joanna was inclined to.

Joanna gazed thoughtfully into her own blue eyes. By this time tomorrow she would be at Raintree Valley, miles away from Gran and the small farm at Hadley where she had spent most of her twenty-one years. She liked animals and being close to the soil; the smell of rain on cabbage leaves, and the cluck of fowls in a sunlit yard. She wasn't afraid of hard work, but she was beginning to feel apprehensive about the Corraines.

She picked up her suitcase and let herself out of the suite. She rode down in the lift to the foyer and asked the clerk to mind her case while she went for a stroll around Hawk's Bay. As she crossed to the swing-doors she looked altogether different from the sturdy, sun-tanned girls who were drifting in and out of the hotel. There had always been an air of retreat about Joanna, an elusive, woodsy quality. Her eyes were the colour of woodsmoke, and she had never yet let a man get close enough to count the various blue tints in her eyes.

A golden bloom of sunshine lay over the bay and brightly-sailed boats were out on the water. She crossed the road and strolled along the promenade, watching the surfers and wondering which one of them was Vance Corraine, who piloted his own plane and who would fly her the rest of the way to the valley. She paused to buy a pineapple ice-cream and heard the laughter of a girl ring out down on the beach. A carefree-looking girl like Viviana, who waved an arm as a sun-dark figure rode in on a great blue swirl of water.

Joanna watched him. He was like a Delphi bronze, his skin agleam from the water and the sunshine. His feet gripped the board and his teeth were a flash of white as the huge wave tried to buck him, and failing lashed him with spray.

'Vance . . .' the name sang on the spray and the blonde girl laughed again. 'Is there nothing, Vance, that can rock you off your feet?'

'A roller is nothing to a scrub bull and I've thrown plenty of those,' he laughed back. 'I'm a Corraine!'

Joanna caught the ring of arrogance in his voice as she turned away and retraced her steps to the hotel, where she sat in the lounge behind a potted palm and a magazine and waited – rather tensely – for sundown.

The hot sun outside had given way to cool shadows when Vance Corraine entered the lounge in search of Joanna. The wall-lights caught the pale sheen of her hair as she glanced up and met for the first time the quizzical impact of his eyes. Dark blue eyes with rather heavy eyelids and a sweep of light brown hair above them. There was an air of leisure about him now; of the sun deep in his pores and a sea-light captive in his gaze. A white dinner-jacket sat easily on his square shoulders and he was smoking a cigarette.

'You must be Joanna Dowling,' he said, and she remembered his voice from the beach, deep and assured and rather more cultured than one expected a cattleman's voice to be. He also made her name sound like Darling, and a tinge of colour crept into her cheeks.

'You must be Mr. Corraine.' She rose to her feet, her fingers clenched on her magazine as she felt the brush of his eyes over her slender figure. She saw in them a flicker of amused surprise, and supposed that she would seem a contrast to his statuesque girl-friend of the beach.

'Shall we have a drink in here before going in to dinner?' he asked. 'I guess you want to ask me a few questions about Raintree and the cocktail bar can get a trifle noisy as the beach crowd drift in.'

'Yes, I am intrigued by Raintree Valley,' she admitted, and she broke into the slight smile that crinkled her eyes. 'And I imagine you have a few questions to ask me, Mr. Corraine.'

'Yes,' he narrowed his eyes against the smoke of his cigarette. 'You wrote in your letter to my aunt that you were used to domestic work and helping around a small farm. I hope, Miss Dowling, that you were telling the truth.'

'The truth?' she exclaimed, and annoyance mingled with amusement that he should doubt the veracity of a girl reared by a stern countrywoman. 'I can do more than tell a cow from a horse, Mr. Corraine. I can bake a batch of bread, whitewash a barn, feed pigs and toss turnips. I wonder if you can do as much?'

He quirked an eyebrow at her comeback, and then he laughed, and it was one of the most attractive sounds she had heard. A trifle mocking and indulgent, and a little throaty. 'I plead guilty to never having tossed a turnip – but you see, Miss Dowling,' again he made it sound like Darling! 'you look too fragile and cool to last for long in the hot sun of our territory. We're way up where the tropics begin, did you know that?'

'I suspected it,' she said dryly. 'Raintrees grows where

it's hot, don't they?'

'English wild flowers don't,' he said, with a glint in his eyes. 'Facing tropic temperatures and the Corraines as well might make you wilt.'

'Are the Corraines so formidable?'

'I think I'd better get you a drink before I answer that one.' He turned to the waiter who had just served a couple who were sitting together in a corner of the lounge – honeymooners, Joanna was willing to bet, from the way the girl couldn't take her eyes off the young man's face.

'As you're a farm girl, I'd better order for you,' drawled Vance Corraine.

'I'd like a gin and pineapple,' she said in a cool voice.

'Fond of pineapples?'

'Very.'

'We grow them up at Raintree.' He gave their order to the waiter, and Joanna sat down on the banquette and smoothed the soft pleats of her dress. She had bought the dress in London and the skirt revealed her slim legs in seamless nylons. Her feet were small in kid casuals, and she felt Vance Corraine looking her over from her ankles to her ash-blonde hair.

'I don't think I ought to take you to Raintree,' he drawled.

Her eyes flashed to his sun-tanned face. 'Your aunt is hiring me to help around the house, not the stockyards, Mr. Corraine.'

'You speak up for yourself, don't you?' He sat down beside her and rested an elbow on the back of the seat so that he faced her. He was lean and attractive in his white dinner-jacket, and his eyes were so deeply blue that the pupils were like sparks. Points of sunshine or fire. A man no girl could ignore.

'Aunt Charly likes people to have a bit of spirit in them,' he added with a smile.

Joanna sat tense on the banquette, without leaning back. If she did so her shoulders would come in contact with his arm, and she was already close enough to this vital Australian. 'You think your aunt will like me, and yet you imply that I won't be suitable for the job she is offering. I'm a little puzzled, Mr. Corraine.'

'Did you know, Miss Dowling, that your eyes change from blue to smoke when you're puzzled?'

'I haven't made a particular study of my eyes,' she rejoined. 'I would prefer to discuss this job, for which I have travelled all the way from Sydney. In her letter Miss Corraine seemed perfectly satisfied with my qualifications, which I do assure you are quite good.'

He laughed again. 'I like a sense of humour, but it isn't for me to say you're good, or for my aunt. It's the Boss who does the hiring and the firing.'

'The Boss?' she echoed. 'But—'

'Adam Corraine, my cousin, who runs the whole of Raintree and a couple of other stations some miles from the homestead. Once-Lonely and Wandaday are not so big, but we muster the cattle at one or the other when the "fats" are ready for transport to the cities in the big trailers we now use instead of droving all the way and running the fat off the cows. They feed for months up on the Raintree hills, where the land is fertile and grassy, and then comes the big drive down to Once-Lonely or Wandaday.'

The names were fascinating, but it was the name of Vance Corraine's cousin that held Joanna's attention. 'I thought—' Her throat had gone rather dry and she was glad to accept her drink and ease the dryness.

'You thought I was in charge of things up at Raintree?'

14

Vance looked quizzical as he swallowed most of his cocktail. 'I'm Adam's offsider. That is to say I share the management of the stations, but he's the Boss. We've both lived at Raintree all our lives, but Adam was trained by our grandfather, Kingsley Corraine, to run things after he died. You see, Joanna, my father was the Prodigal Son who took his portion and spent it in the gay city. Adam's father worked day and night for the old man, and then came the war and he was called to the colours. He died out in Burma and the old man turned to Adam and never let him alone until he lived, breathed and thought of nothing but making Raintree and its mustering stations the envy of Queensland. When King died, as everyone called the old man, I fell in line as Adam's second in command. King always said that I had the charm, and Adam the arm.'

Vance looked at the drink in his hand and there was a small twist of a smile at the edge of his mouth. 'I suppose it could be said that Adam takes after the old man and that pride in Raintree is in his bones.'

Joanna met the dark blue eyes, and she felt a stirring of antagonism against the man she had never met, who had the power to let her stay at Raintree or be sent away, back to the city and the crowds where someone like herself could feel far more lonely than in the country. She was used to the countryside. To waking to bird song, and to filling a farmhouse kitchen with the smell of freshly baked bread.

She wasn't in the least fragile . . . while Adam Corraine sounded as hard as sandstone.

'Adam of the stony bones, with his thoughts in the clouds,' she said tartly. 'I'm not afraid of your cousin, Mr. Corraine.'

'You've never met him!'

'True,' she said. 'But at least give me the chance to do so.'

'You've got grit, haven't you, Joanna Dowling.' He rose to his feet and held out a hand to her. 'Let's go in to dinner and I'll let you tell me all about yourself.'

His fingers were warm and strong about hers, and people looked at them when they entered the restaurant with its indirect lighting and its soft music. Vance was nonchalant, as if accustomed to being recognized as one of the mighty Corraines. But Joanna felt shy. She was unused to smart places like this, and hovering waiters, and she tried to recover a little poise behind the shield of a large menu.

After they had ordered their meal, the wine steward hovered at Vance's elbow and after a few moments' consultation he said to her: 'Do you like champagne?'

'I've never had it,' she said, and she caught the flash of amusement in the dark blue eyes as he turned to the waiter to order a bottle. For a cattleman he was well up on the vintages of wine, and once again Joanna was assailed by a sense of wonderment. If the suave Vince Corraine was manager up at Raintree, whatever was the Boss like?

Their wine was brought to them, with the lobster in the cracked shell which Vance had said she would like. Flute champagne glasses were placed on the table and she watched as the cork was unwired, making a popping sound as it emerged looking like a small mushroom. The golden wine creamed into the slender glasses, and then they were alone and Vance raised his glass. '*C'est la guerre,*' he smiled.

'Yes.' She felt the nose-prickling, sparkly bubbles as she took a sip of the champagne and found it not sweet but slightly tart and delicious. 'I think I'm going to need all my courage, after what you've told me about your cousin.'

'Tell me about yourself.' Vance took hold of a tiny fork and showed her how to coax the pieces of lobster out of the shell. These were dipped in a smooth sauce that blended perfectly with the fish.

Joanna drank some more wine and found that it made conversation very easy. The soft music also helped, and the scent of a night flower that stole in through the open window beside their table. She talked of the farm, and of Viviana, and of the journey that had brought her among strangers when she had hoped to see her twin sister, and to live and work in Sydney with her.

'So you were the stay-at-home sister?' said Vance. 'How does it feel to be out in the great big world – and Australia is very big?'

'It feels – bewildering,' she admitted. 'The country place I come from is small and placid, where the same sort of things happen each day, and where you feel safe because there are no real surprises.'

'Is that all you ever wanted, Joanna Dowling, to feel safe?' Vance Corraine quizzed her face and looked into her wide eyes, with their changing tints that made them rather mysterious. Her skin had the warm pallor associated with flowers, and her smooth ash-blonde hair rested quiet against the slender nape of her neck. She was the pastel of which Viviana was the portrait. In contrast to her vivid twin she had always thought of herself as plain, but each time Vance spoke her name and made it sound like Darling, colour ran under her skin and she was in the same danger as unplucked flowers.

'Some of us feel a sense of duty, Mr. Corraine, and I couldn't leave my grandmother while she needed me. The farm was small, and we had a lad to help us, but it would have been too much for Gran to manage if I hadn't stayed until she retired.'

'But in your heart you longed for new horizons, eh?'

'I . . . I suppose I must have done.' Joanna fingered the stem of her wine glass and smiled a little. 'Perhaps at heart I'm more like Viviana than I realize. She always goes after the things she wants and gets them, and I want this job at Raintree Valley.'

'I wonder why?' Vance bent his brown head to his plate of tenderloin steak, garden spinach and a large potato baked in its jacket.

'It's the name,' she said a trifle defensively. He might guess that she liked him! He was very attractive, but she sensed also that he was rather dangerous. A man who could ride the waves as he did; who was part of a ménage that owned three big stations founded by a man called King, was far from ordinary. And Joanna was far from home!

'You aren't intimidated by what I've told you about my cousin Adam?' Vance glanced up slowly and caught her wide gaze upon him.

'He sounds an autocrat, but I'm sure of my own capabilities and I want the chance to prove them.' Joanna stabbed little green peas on to her fork and ate them with a piece of golden fried chicken. 'You won't deny me that chance, will you, Mr. Corraine?'

'I wouldn't want to deny you anything, Miss Darling.'

'It's spelled DOW,' she rejoined.

'I guessed it was.' He looked directly at her and there was a persuasive charm to his smile. 'If my accent does odd things to your name, then you'd better allow me to call you Joanna.'

18

'But we've only just met,' she protested.

'Out here we all use first names – Joanna. There's a lot of land, a lot of cattle, and not so many people. We like to be friendly because unlike folks in the cities we don't keep running into our neighbours. We often only know them by name, for our contact is by radio-transmitter.'

His smile was quizzical. 'That's something you don't know about, the loneliness of a place such as Raintree. Of being miles from the nearest town, of depending on a radio doctor, of needing just the sound of a woman's voice.'

'I can learn to know about it,' she said. 'It isn't as if I'm a city girl, and I did explain in my letter to your aunt that I was from England and would need a little time to adjust to the routine of an Australian homestead. She made no bones about this in her reply and seemed eager for an English home-help.'

'Aunt Charly came from England years ago and remains nostalgic about the old country. The point is,' Vance waited as the waiter refilled their glasses, 'had Adam not been away at Once-Lonely seeing to the installation of a new roof – it was King's first station and is quite old – he'd have vetted her replies to applicants for the job.'

'And you don't think I'd have stood much chance?' Joanna broke in. 'Because I'm a greenhorn and a stranger I might upset the smooth running of Raintree and that would upset the Boss. You spoke about the loneliness, Mr. Corraine. Perhaps your aunt is lonely and feels in need of someone English to tell her about things over there, and to talk herself about the places she once knew. Surely Adam Corraine allows people to be human and vulnerable?'

Vance Corraine smiled at her outburst. 'A long time

ago King lost his temper with Adam and cracked his stockman's whip across the shoulders that were still a stripling's. Adam grabbed that whip and slung it down a bore, and no one has ever seen him look so furious, or so nakedly hurt. Nothing since that day feels the whip on Corraine property, but nobody has ever got close again to Adam. He's got the arm, and it's strong and long and everyone is kept at the length of that arm.'

'He sounds rather aloof,' Joanna murmured, and she felt startled by the way she had winced, almost hearing the crack of the stockman's whip across Adam Corraine's shoulders. It brought home forcibly to her the toughness of these people; the basic differences of their outlook and their life on the big livestock stations of this wide land.

'Maybe he doesn't realize that your Aunt Charlotte is lonely,' she added. 'He may be so involved in his work, and his ambitions for Raintree, that he's lost contact with people more vulnerable than himself.'

'That is one of the dangers for women out here,' Vance admitted. 'The men always have plenty to occupy them, but the women are tied to the homestead, and being a long way from their neighbours they can't drop in on them for a gossip over a cup of tea. Aunt Charly is still pretty active for her age and has cultivated a marvellous garden – it's Bonney who gets lonely.'

'Bonney is the young person mentioned in your aunt's advertisement?' Joanna asked.

'Bonney is eighteen,' Vance said rather drawlingly. 'The Boss provided a home for her when her parents lost their lives in a flood about four years ago. Bonney was at boarding-school in Melbourne and Adam sort of adopted her, having been a friend of her father's. I have a notion Aunt Charly is beginning to find her a bit of a handful. Are you up to handling young fillies who know they're darned pretty?'

'Is she very pretty?' Joanna smiled, remembering Viviana and the handful she had been, with her outbursts of temperament and her flirtations in the orchard. She had been bored by the farm and there had been nothing Gran or Joanna could do to please her.

Perhaps Charlotte Corraine was worried in case Adam's pretty ward took it into her head to run away?

'You're forgetting my twin and how headstrong she was.' Joanna tasted her banana cream pie and found it delicious. 'Are you going to take me to Raintree Valley so I can meet your cousin and at least get a hearing?'

'What will you do, Joanna, if he turns you down?'

'I shall be very disappointed.'

'Because you're intrigued by Raintree and its occupants, eh?' Vance leaned back in his seat and studied Joanna through narrowed blue eyes. 'You're a romantic, Joanna, and you look as soft as chinchilla. The Boss is expecting a hefty wench who's not only used to home-helping, but who can act as riding companion for Bonney.'

'I learned how to handle a horse when I was still at school,' Joanna broke in. 'Our farm was quite close to the Hadley riding stables.'

'Our range horses are rather more spirited than your country lane ponies,' Vance mocked. 'Nothing out here is really tame, you know. Not man or beast.'

'If I had been the timid sort, Mr. Corraine, I wouldn't have left England at all. Surely that fact is in my favour if everything else is against it? I'm not chicken even if I don't look tough—'

'I'm perfectly happy with the way you look, Joanna.'

She looked at Vance and then away again, for his smile was slow, attractive, a little dangerous to a girl who was far from home and whose fate seemed to rest in the hands of a stranger she didn't like the sound of. If only Vance Corraine had been the master of Raintree!

'Do you want coffee, or a stroll in the garden?' he asked half teasingly. He didn't wait for her reply, as if aware that she would turn timid and ask for coffee. He rose to his feet and held out a hand to her and meeting the glint of challenge in his eyes, she placed her hand in the warm, strong palm, roughened from riding but good to feel. She was confused as he drew her to her feet. She was close to him for a moment and very aware of how sun-tanned he was in contrast to his white jacket. How tall and unafraid of life.

'You almost turned scared just then,' he teased, his fingers locked firmly about hers as he led her out to the terrace through long french doors. The music faded a little, but the scent of the nightflowers grew stronger. He lounged against a tree, still holding her hand and looking at it as if amused by its smallness. 'Did you leave any boyfriends behind in England?'

'Dozens,' she said lightly.

'If that were the case, then you wouldn't be so shy of me – yes, you are, Joanna! You're scared right now in case I kiss you. I bet you've never been kissed by a man.'

She looked at Vance with large eyes, wondering what it would be like to feel the hard warmth of his arms around her, holding back the night, holding her close to his carefree heart in the kind of kiss he had probably given to dozens of girls. No, she wouldn't be added to his list of conquests! No man was going to kiss her just because the stars were shining and the frangipani was sweet. The man who kissed her for the first time was going to want that kiss more than anything else in the world.

'I had no idea that cattlemen were such accomplished flirts,' she said. 'I thought they were always out on the range mustering cattle.'

'Flirting with an attractive girl is something that comes natural to a man,' he said, and she felt his left hand steal up her arm to her shoulder. 'You're all tense, Joanna, as if you can't forget your grandma's advice about how dangerous young men can be. It's a sweet danger, you know, and part of being alive.'

'And you're flirting with me, Mr. Corraine, because you think I won't get taken on at Raintree. Adam Corraine sounds the sort who wouldn't like his cousin to be on kissing terms with the home-help!'

Vance let her go and reached up a lazy hand to a cluster of creamy stars. 'You've a lot of cool nerve, haven't you, Joanna Dowling? Are you cool all the way through – the original icy Saxon?'

'I'm sensible,' she rejoined, knowing it to be a word most men hated; probably the most off-putting thing a girl could be. 'My sister Viviana is the one who sparkles. She is the champagne blonde in our family.'

'Dizzy and bubbly?' he drawled. 'Pretty as paint?'

'Yes, but she also knows what she wants and I'm certain she'll make a big name for herself one of these days. She has personality.'

'And what do you want out of life, Joanna?' He took out his cigarette case and offered it, but she shook her head and watched as the flame of his lighter illuminated his lean face and revealed those tiny twinkles deep in his eyes. By the flame he looked at her, and then the lighter clicked shut and the smoke of his cigarette mingled with the scent of semi-tropical flowers.

She had not thought of Australia as a romantic land, but it was, in a subtle, disturbing way. From here the pounding sea could be heard, bringing with it thoughts of the Great Barrier Reef, on which lay coral islands. The stars clustered in shining groups and the fronds of palm and gum trees bowed against the dark sky.

Joanna had never given much thought to what she wanted. She was not ambitious like Viviana, but here in this new land she was aware of a new restlessness, a desire without a name.

'I suppose like most people I want – happiness,' she murmured.

'Can happiness be defined, Joanna?' There was in his voice a sudden note of seriousness, and she wondered why. Surely Vance Corraine had most of the things that brought happiness? His position at Raintree was secure and he probably earned very good money. He was intelligent, attractive and able to participate in the joys of life. She couldn't think of anything he lacked – unless it was a wife, and men like Vance were usually happier without ties.

'Happiness is a bubble,' she said lightly. 'Shimmering and then gone for a while.'

'Elusive, eh?' The tiny pulse of his cigarette grew bright and then dimmed. 'Have you ever flown in a plane through the small, still hours separating midnight from the dawn?'

'No.' Her heart beat fast as she looked at him, his jacket a white blur, his mouth faintly outlined by the glow of his cigarette. She saw his lips curve in a smile, and suddenly it amazed her that she had known this man so short a while. She felt there was something about him that she had known for a long time. It was as if they had met in a dream, but as if in that dream he had differed in various ways from the reality.

It was a strange feeling, and she put it down to her long

journey ending in a garden under the stars.

'Joanna, we're going to fly among the stars tonight, and you'll see Raintree Valley as the dawn breaks on the sandstone hills and turns them lion-gold. Perhaps I'm cruel to let you have your first glimpse of Raintree in this way, because you're the kind of girl to fall in love with a place at first sight—'

'Cruel because Adam Corraine might not want me at Raintree?'

'You said you were willing to face that possibility, because Adam as I know him is a man who takes what he wants for Raintree, who discards without hesitation what he doesn't want.'

'Adam of the stony bones,' she murmured, with a feeling in her heart that he was a man who was easier to hate than to love. A man of too much pride in property, which a stockman's whip had sealed into his hard bones.

Suddenly Joanna was unsure ... if to see Raintree was to love the place, then it might be better if she didn't fly there with Vance.

He moved and she felt the brush of his arm. He gripped her by the chin and tilted her face up to him. 'Don't lose heart, Joanna Dowling, girl with the smoke-tinted eyes and pale gold hair. If my cousin won't let you stay at Raintree, then I'll marry you.'

She heard the note of humour in his voice and knew he jested, but all the same she drew away from him with a laughing gasp. 'You shouldn't go around making proposals of that sort,' she said breathlessly. 'One day a girl will bite and you'll be landed with a wife you don't really want.'

'Joanna, don't you ever act on impulse?' he laughed.

'I'm too sensible, I told you!'

'You?' He laughed again and ran a caressing finger

25

down her cheek. 'You're about as sensible as an over-grown joey in its mother's pouch. You're a little scared of me, so I just don't know how you're going to cope with Adam.'

She didn't know herself, but that was something she didn't have to think about until tomorrow.

Tonight she was going to have the unusual experience of flying among the stars above Queensland, and her pilot would be this young man with the sun-browned, dare-devil face, and the light of humour in his dark blue eyes. Not a man to be taken seriously, but at the same time with something very disturbing about him.

'Is your plane a large one?' she asked.

'It's a two-seater monoplane,' he said as they began to make their way back to the hotel. 'I call her Bony-Bird, but she's game and carries a fair amount of cargo. Supplies needed at Raintree, where we're cut off by over a hundred miles from the nearest town. The mail comes in by plane, and also the doctor when he's needed, but for the most part we're a community on our own. It's almost feudal, Joanna, like the old castle settlements of the days of the knights, and Adam is the overlord.'

'And who are you?' she smiled. 'Sir Vance of the valley?'

They reached the terrace and as she glanced up at him the soft lighting shone on his face and left shadow in the cleft of his chin. His white jacket gave a silvery impression and it wasn't so very far-fetched that he was like a knight who was going to carry her off to the castle.

'Joanna,' he smiled, 'you are dangerously romantic.'

CHAPTER TWO

DAYLIGHT brimmed and roused Joanna from the sleep into which she had fallen.

'There's coffee in that flask behind you.' Vance shot her a smile as she stirred and opened her eyes, and turned up to him a bemused face framed by her tousled fair hair. 'Pour out a couple of mugs – soon we'll be over the valley.'

'I fell asleep,' she said drowsily.

'Yes,' his eyes held hers a brief moment, 'on my shoulder.'

'Oh—' Somewhat confused, she found the flask of coffee in the satchel he had brought on board last night, along with the roast beef sandwiches they had consumed during the starlit hours of the flight. It had been a strange, magical experience, and Joanna felt the fast beating of her heart as she realized that it was almost over and soon they would be landing on the private airstrip at Raintree.

The coffee had kept nice and hot and it awoke Joanna fully to the scenery they were flying above. She saw the jungle that padded the sides of a mountain range, a rich green denseness where rivers shone like strips of silver, belted by dark mangroves in which lurked the huge, old-as-rock crocodiles.

'It's a real jungle,' said Vance, 'alive with clinging vines, stinging trees and great fruit bats. The stinging tree is as vicious as its name and hides from the unwary among large ferns and pretty creepers. Quite a place for a hunting trip, but I prefer the open range where you can

27

see the bulls when they come at you with fire in their eye.'

He laughed at the wide-eyed look Joanna was giving him. 'I warned you that we're an untamed lot at Raintree. We're miles from anywhere and life goes on – except for a few mechanical changes – much as it did when the first Corraine out fom England crossed the land by wagon. He had his young wife with him and their first son was born on the trek.'

'You're proud of being tough and self-sufficient, aren't you, Vance?' His name came to her lips more easily now, for it seemed ridiculously formal to address by his surname a man with whom she had flown among the stars, and whose shoulder had pillowed her head while she slept.

'It's in the blood, Joanna. We couldn't live any other kind of life. When Adam and I were still quite small we went on droving trips with King. We learned young about the night riding, ringing the cattle and singing the old ballads to keep them calm. Sleeping in a swag by a campfire. Knowing the hot gold days, and how cold it could blow at night.'

'You also seemed very much at home in the water at Hawk's Bay.' She looked at his profile and remembered the clean, tanned lines of his body sprayed by the silvery blue water.

'You saw me?' he exclaimed.

'Yes, I watched you riding the waves. There was a girl waiting for you on the beach.'

'A stockman on leave has to relax, Joanna.' He looked at her out of the tail of his eye.

'Of course,' she said, smiling to herself. 'What I mean is that you're far more sophisticated than I imagined.'

'People rarely are the way we imagine them.' He

grinned. 'The Boss is in for a shaker when he sees you – look below, Joanna, we're flying over the herds!'

She peered from the cockpit window and there far below was a moving mass of roan hides against the sun-tipped grassy hills. So many that she caught her breath in awe. Among them rode the horsemen, looking from this height like toy figures.

'I've never seen anything like it,' she gasped. 'Isn't it frightening to be on horseback in that mob of cattle?'

'You get used to it,' he chuckled. 'Droving is the hardest job, when it's hot and dusty and the mob gets restless and the next waterhole might be dried out. Things have been easier, though, since Adam decided to ship by road from the other stations. King wouldn't like all the mechanization, but you've got to keep up with the times and the cattle get to market with plenty of meat still left on them.'

'The men begin work early,' Joanna remarked, for the sun had not long risen above the mountains.

'And get most of it behind them by noon, when the sun is high and we relax for a siesta. Now we're flying right over the valley, Joanna! See those sandstone cliffs and the gorge ... there's a bridge across it leading to the house, and back of the house, like a great wild garden, there's a rain-forest. The valley, the forest, and all the surrounding land belongs to the Corraines. This is our world. No one gets in unless we allow them in.'

'Like the Doones,' she said wonderingly, and thought of the girl Bonney who felt lonely here. For what was she lonely, when she lived among all this wild beauty? The city and the bright lights? The shops, restaurants and gaiety beloved of Joanna's own sister?

Vance circled right round the valley before coming down on the runway a couple of miles from the house, with fronded trees of a tropical look lining the strip and bowing in the breeze created by the passage of the plane.

'Here we are.' Vance turned from the controls and quirked an eyebrow when he found Joanna smoothing her hair into her chignon and assuming again her unruffled look. 'Y'know, I rather like you with your hair out of place,' he drawled.

'It's your cousin I've got to impress. There, I'm made all new.' She patted her hair, dropped her lipstick and comb into her bag and smiled at Vance before glancing away from his intent look. She wore a sheep-lined canvas jacket he had loaned her for the flight and it was too big for her, so that she looked rather helpless in it. Sunshine lit the cockpit and her hair and skin were very fair . . . she had an untouched look and Vance leaned forward as if she drew him like a magnet.

'It's none of Adam's business if I want to fraternize with the home-help,' he said wickedly.

'I've not been hired yet.' She drew back from him, alarmed because the cockpit was small and he was broad across the shoulders, and his eyes were the dark blue of a deep, drowning sea. 'Hadn't we better get out?' she asked nervously.

'Are you so anxious to meet Adam?'

'Strong medicine is best swallowed quickly, as my grandmother would say.'

'The medicine upon this occasion might not have a beneficial effect.' He fingered the sheep's wool collar against her throat. 'Do you remember what I said last night, if Adam turned you down?'

'That was so much nonsense,' she scoffed. 'Champagne bubbles.'

'Want me to prove that it wasn't all champagne?' He came even nearer and Joanna was holding him off with her hands against his shoulders when a fistful of small stones rattled against the cockpit window. Vance glanced round and there on the runway below the plane stood a man waving his arms about.

'No peace for the wicked,' Vance growled. 'The boys want to unload the cargo, and I suppose I'd better take you to meet the Boss. He isn't like me, Joanna – except maybe to look at, in a sundown light. What I mean is—'

'I know what you mean.' Her heart was beating in her throat. 'He won't make allowances for the fact that I'm far from home, or that I have blonde hair.'

Vance grinned. 'You have grit and a sense of humour, Joanna. I could marry a gal so gallant.'

'Marriage is a serious business, Mr. Corraine. You don't take it up like golf or polo, and drop it if you find it bores you. It's a relationship meant to last a lifetime.'

'Alas, a girl with ideals!' His smile was wickedly attractive. 'We make our own hell, eh? Someone else has to make our heaven?'

'That's love, isn't it?' she said simply.

'It sounds great, if it's for the finding.' He swung open the cockpit and the sudden warmth of the sun and the tang of Raintree caught at Joanna as she followed Vance out of the plane. The men who had come to unload the cases of provisions and machine parts stared at her, a slim figure in a canvas jacket over a pleated dress, there against the wasp-gold of the monoplane. There was no doubt in any of the eyes that looked at her that nobody like her had been seen at Raintree for many years. Her fair, reserved looks were utterly English, and her wide eyes were inquiring yet shy as she looked about her and realized that she was actually at Raintree.

The men looked dumbfounded, and then into the silence broke the sound of pounding hooves and heads turned to watch the rapidly approaching horseman.

Joanna blinked as the blue and gold of the sky dazzled her eyes, and then she heard someone say, 'It's the Boss — better start getting them crates out of the plane!'

Vance had lit himself a cigarette and now he stood with a thumb in his belt. The pounding of Joanna's heart blended with that of the hooves as the raking chestnut galloped down the runway as if it were a racetrack, to be pulled up just short of the plane, the girl, and the cluster of men, who set to work at once unloading the cargo. The rider sat there, leaning his arms on the pommel of his saddle, while the chestnut flung up its head and made a huffing sound through proud, arching nostrils. Any man who could handle that horse was iron-fisted, Joanna thought.

'Hi there, Vance,' he said, and all the time he looked at Joanna with eyes that seemed to have a light inside them, alert and raking, like the play of lightning. He wore a slouch hat, check shirt and white trousers, and then with a supple deliberation he slid from the back of his horse and held the reins coiled over his left arm as he slowly pushed his hat to the back of his forehead and the sun flared across assertive, sunbitten features, and showed the sunburned brows above the silvery eyes.

He was alarmingly tall and tough as rawhide. The sort of man who liked his heels in the earth and his face to the sky. Boss of Raintree, a man in unshakeable command of himself!

'You took your time getting back to Raintree.' He flashed a look at his cousin, and Joanna was startled by the quick flash of resemblance between them. Vance shrugged and lifted his cigarette to his lips.

'Adam, this is Joanna Dowling,' he said. 'The girl who has come to help out at the house.'

Joanna stood very still, at the mercy of her nerves and trying not to show it. This was not a man who would have any patience with feminine fears . . . it wouldn't matter to him that he scared the daylights out of her.

'I take it this young lady kept you so busy at Hawk's Bay,' he said to Vance, 'that you forgot we needed that new dynamo for the bore at Once-Lonely!'

'I didn't forget, and Joanna didn't get in on the bus until yesterday. I had to wait delivery of the dynamo—'

'Joanna?' Adam Corraine quirked a sunburned eyebrow, but unlike Vance he looked dangerous instead of quizzically attractive. 'Well, Miss Darling, you should have saved yourself a long trip for nothing. I don't employ helpless young things up here at Raintree, no matter how strong my cousin's wish that I would—'

'I'm not!' she broke in, finding her voice and utterly confirmed in her opinion that he was arrogant and hateful. 'I'm not helpless – and the name is DOWLING!'

'Oh, do forgive me.' He smiled deliberately, showing hard white teeth. 'About the name, I mean – it really sounded as if my cousin called you darling.'

She quivered with dislike and her fingers clenched the strap of her shoulder-bag. 'As I explained to your cousin, Mr. Corraine, I have lived and worked on a farm since I was a child, and it would at least be a little gracious of you to give me a trial before judging me. I do happen to know which end of a cow to milk and I'm quite at home in a kitchen.'

'I have a large crew who need feeding several times a day, Miss Dowling, and I can't see you spoiling those pale hands in buckets of vegetables, or plucking fowls with them and kneading dough for the bread. The baker doesn't call each morning, this far afield, and often there are two dozen eggs to fry with the steaks my bachelor lads like for breakfast. The rest who have wives eat at their own bungalows, of course. And that is the job! To help out in the kitchen and the house, and maybe ride an hour each day with my ward, and match her in a game of tennis.'

He seemed, from the glint in his sky-grey eyes, to get immense satisfaction out of listing the requirements of the job, and there forked through Joanna a stab of hatred for this autocrat who had probably had things all his own way ever since Kingsley Corraine had died and left him in charge of Raintree and its outlying stations. She wanted to tell him to keep the job, yet on the other hand she wanted to prove that she was up to it.

She tilted her chin and met squarely his challenging eyes. 'Are you a gambling man, Mr. Corraine?' she asked.

His left brow slanted and Vance gave a cough as he caught cigarette smoke in his throat.

'I'm an Australian,' Adam Corraine drawled.

'Then take a gamble on me,' she challenged him. 'If you've got the nerve to let me prove you wrong – for once.'

'Young woman,' his mouth looked dangerous for a moment, and then he gave a sardonic laugh, 'you're a bit of a cool one, aren't you, to match those looks of yours! What sort of a farm was it you lived on – poultry, a couple of cows, some cabbages and fruit?'

'Yes.' She felt stung by the note of lofty amusement in his voice, but remembering the ocean of cattle she and Vance had flown over, she supposed a couple of cows and a hen coop would seem amusing. 'It might have been a smallholding, but we worked, my grandmother and I, to get a living out of it.'

His eyes flicked her ash-blonde hair, which she wore madonna-style because her hair was of a fine-soft texture that looked childish if she didn't keep it controlled. It was also a style that made her look far more poised than she felt.

'Okay,' there was a sardonic twist to Adam Corraine's mouth, 'you can stay for a fortnight, but if you don't suit and can't fit into the swing of things, then Vance will fly you back to Hawk's Bay, where you should have no trouble getting a job in a boutique or one of the hotels that cater for tourists.'

'Do you think that's all I'm really suited for?' she asked indignantly.

'You're not used to the big country and not everyone can take to it.' He held her eyes, made her aware of the sheer vitality of his gaze. 'In all frankness, Miss Dowling, I would prefer a girl of our own kind at the homestead. The boys will hang round you because you're something new, and I don't want any fights or trouble over a female.'

'I assure you—'

'Assure me of nothing,' he broke in, a ring of hardness in his voice. 'Thirty-three years have taught me that if you let yourself be soft about anything then you're in for trouble, one way or another. Common sense tells me to pack you off back to the bay, but my aunt's letter led you to think you'd be suitable, so in all fairness I've got to give you a trial.'

'I don't want you to strain yourself, Mr. Corraine,' she said frigidly.

Vance, who had evidently been straining himself not to laugh at Joanna's daring, now gave way to a chortle that made the other men look over at the Boss and the girl, and then at each other. The situation didn't take much summing up . . . a catalyst had arrived at Raintree in the shape of a slim, fair, cool-skinned Britisher.

Vance drove her up to the house in a jeep, through the honey warmth of the sun that now lay over the morning. She still felt rather shaken up by her first encounter with the Boss and she sat silent beside Vance, seeing the gum trees and casuarinas that shaded the hilly drive to the homestead, the bright flash of birds like bunches of petals on the wing.

'Rosellas,' Vance murmured.

She came out of her dream and looked at him. 'Oh – you mean the birds?'

'Yes, the birds. Those full of chatter are galahs.'

'They're a pretty colour, that mixture of dove-grey and pink.'

'You seem overcome by your first meeting with Adam.'

'Is he always so – brusque?'

'Yes, with strangers – especially if they happen to be women.'

'Is he a misogynist?'

'No – I sometimes think he's shy.'

'Shy?' Joanna exclaimed.

'Some men can face a mob of stampeding cattle and not blink an eyelash, but when it comes to a slip of a girl—' Vance swung the jeep round a bend in the road. 'I told you he'd reckon you as just a corn dolly.'

'Nerve!' she muttered. 'The implication that I'm suited for nothing but selling beachwear and volley balls!'

'It might be easier work, Joanna, than being a home-help. And if you were at Hawk's Bay I could come in on flying visits.'

Her gaze dwelt on the deep, rich valley above which

they were driving, filled with green shadow and birds and the bright sparkle of streams. She compared it to the holiday bay filled with people and knew she could be happy here ... if only Adam Corraine would have the patience to let her get used to everything. Shy of women indeed! He was too self-governed to care what other people thought of him ... he was the Boss of Raintree!

He was the favoured grandson of the man who had been the uncrowned king of all this territory. Favoured because he was harder, more ambitious, less likely to care for people more than property.

She looked at Vance and again her liking for him flooded over her. He might bear a fleeting resemblance to his cousin, but he was much the nicer of the two.

'The valley is beautiful,' she murmured. 'Like Shangri-la.'

'It's the valley of the wail when the wind is blowing.'

She took a deep breath of the air that had a buoyancy in it, as if champagne tickled her nose. Vance slowed the jeep and directed her attention to a blue gum tree and a pair of koalas playing in the branches and nibbling the tips of the leaves. They had black-button noses, innocent eyes, and a furry teddy-bear look. 'Cute, eh?' Vance smiled at Joanna. 'Cuddly and trusting, and they never bite.'

'I must take a snap of them!' She leaned over to the back seat to open her suitcase, in which her small camera was tucked down in a corner. She felt Vance's hand against her waist, holding her as she adjusted the camera and took a picture of the koalas.

'You'll see dozens of them around the homestead,' he laughed.

'I want to send snaps to Gran,' she explained, sliding down into her seat. 'If she sees what a lovely place Raintree is, then she won't imagine that I'm somewhere at the back of beyond and in danger from wild men.'

'But, Joanna,' he leaned near and the breath of a kiss brushed her cheek, 'this is the back of beyond, and the Corraines do have wild blood in them.'

She looked into his eyes that were the deep blue of evening skies – unlike Adam's, that were like the sky early in the morning, cool and clear and silvery.

'Are those wide white gates the entrance to the station?' She pointed along the road.

'Yes, those are the gates of the kingdom,' he jested.

As they approached the gates an aborigine boy slid off a rail and swung them wide open. He stared at Joanna, hitched his pants and went back to his perch.

'You should be at school,' Vance called out as they passed through the gates. 'Adoniah will tan your breeches.'

The boy shrugged. 'Don't have to know sums to be stockman,' he retorted.

'Don't you be so sure.' A grin twitched at the corner of Vance's mouth. 'Those cows have got to be counted at the mustering.'

'Boss do that. The Boss do all the figuring.'

'Sure, the Boss is mighty clever, but he had to go to school to get that way.'

The boy looked sceptical, as if in his opinion Adam Corraine's wisdom was a gift of the gods.

'Come on, jump on the running-board and we'll drop you off at school.'

The boy stared again at Joanna and when she smiled at him, he came running across and took a show-off leap on to the running-board at her side of the jeep. His skin was like brown satin and his teeth gleamed rice-white in the shy smile he gave her. She was to learn that Adam Corraine's best stockriders were aborigine men, who lived on the station with their families and had their own houses set among the mango and candelabra trees.

The wooden school building was surrounded by a picket fence and a bronze bell hung in the porch. The sound of the assembly hymn sounded sweet on the morning air as the reluctant pupil entered the school.

'Adoniah Smith is another of our remarkable characters,' smiled Vance. 'He not only runs the school, but he can shoe a horse, play a violin, and grow roses. Roses, Joanna, in this part of the world – deep red ones.'

'I'm beginning to believe that this place is truly Shangri-la.' She looked about her at the bungalows set among the shade trees, at smoothly kept lawns on which cane chairs and tables were set, where children's toys lay bright in the sun, and bits and pieces of washing dried white in the warmth. A tame goose strutted across the buffalo grass, and a slim dark girl waved as they passed by.

'That's Lenita, the Italian wife of one of our stockmen. They've not long had a *bambino*, and is Boye proud of his son!'

Joanna glanced back at the lovely Italian girl, like a picture against a background of red poinciana trees and a coolibah that shaded a child's cradle.

'To be a painter!' Joanna exclaimed. 'One would go beautifully mad trying to get it all down on canvas.'

Vance chuckled. 'Aunt Charly is an inspired amateur. A couple of her paintings adorn the walls of my bungalow.'

'Don't you live with the family up at the house?' Joanna gave him a surprised look, and wondered in that moment if any antagonism lay between him and his cousin Adam.

39

'I prefer a bachelor bungalow,' he said suavely. 'I take my meals up at the homestead, but it suits me better to have my own place with my own things around me. You'll have to call on me, Joanna. I'll make you very welcome.'

She heard him and smiled absently, for most of her attention was upon the building they had come in sight of, the house built long ago by King Corraine and crowning the flat summit of a hill. It rambled as good houses should and had walls aglow with mauve clouds of bougainvillea. It was fronted by the graceful wrought-iron beloved of the Victorians, and slender pillars supported a deep shady veranda that winged around the house with covered ways leading to courts and gardens. The louvred shutters beyond the front veranda were open to let in the breeze, singing now and again through the tall trees. Soon she would know the name of all the trees and meant to know them, but right now she sat bemused as Vance braked the jeep in front of the homestead.

It was so strong and so right, set there on a summit overlooking the valley. A place of cedar and iron and lion-gold stone, its shady veranda rooms overhung by a wide-roofed upper storey. With flowering vines clustering around the pillars, soft veils against the stone, and cane long chairs and rattan tables set about within the veranda, the beams of the cedar retreat from the sun hung with lamps and baskets of flowers.

There the family would sit when the sun went down and the men rode in from the hills. They would watch the stars in the vast, immeasurable sky of this faraway land, and the smell of coffee would mingle with all the scents drifting up from Raintree Valley.

She followed Vance up the steps of the veranda and across to the louvred door that led into the house. The heat faded to coolness in the long, fan-serviced lounge. The walls were panelled in golden bamboo, woven rugs lay on the polished boards of the floor, and there were armchairs with comfortable dents in them. It was a restful room, with one vivid painting of a pearling lugger with her sails set wide against the sea and the sky.

Joanna gave a start – as if out of a dream – as Vance bent to a table and rang the cowbell that stood on it. 'Aunt Charly is probably in the kitchen helping to prepare lunch. The kitchen is way back, but she'll hear the bell. It might take her a few minutes to join us,' Vance added. 'She broke a bone in her foot and it's still in plaster – there, can you hear the sound of her stick?'

It was plain in the stillness that hung over the house, and once again Joanna's heart was beating with the anxiety that she be acceptable in the eyes of a Corraine. Her fingers clenched on the strap of her bag. She didn't know why she cared so much about being wanted here, but it would be unbearable if she encountered again the coolness and the lack of enthusiasm with which Adam Corraine had received her.

The person with the walking stick paused outside the door, and then it was pushed fully open and Charlotte Maud Corraine hobbled into the lounge.

She stared at Joanna with the penetrating eyes of the family. She took in her skin and her wide eyes that had known only the gentle sunshine of Britain, and she nodded to herself in the way of the elderly. 'Yes, you are English to your bones, aren't you?' Charlotte smiled and the shadow of beauty returned to the face that was seamed by the sun and the years and the pioneer life she had known in Australia. Her voice retained its English tones and there was in her manner something of grandness as she invited Joanna to take a chair.

'Your journey has been a long one, Miss Dowling, but I hope a pleasant one. I expect you could do with a cup of tea? Vance, will you go to the kitchen and brew it? Young Tilly has her hands in a bowl of onions.'

Vance smiled and gave his aunt a gallant little bow. 'At your command, Duchess. Neither of us has had breakfast, so I'll scramble some eggs and ham if that's okay?'

'Of course it is, and I do wish you wouldn't use slang.'

'How about strine?' He cocked a lopsided grin at Joanna. 'Do you fancy some baked necks?'

'Baked necks of what?' she asked in bewilderment.

'Bacon and eggs,' he laughed. 'Australians have a habit of running their words together, haven't you noticed?'

'Well, I haven't been here all that long—'

'Stop devilling the young woman and go and make that tea,' his aunt said severely. 'She has only just arrived here and hasn't had time to get used to our outbackish ways. You know where the bacon is hung, and get some new laid eggs out of the nest.'

He sauntered away, leaving Joanna alone with his aunt, who leaned back in her chair after propping her plastered foot on a hassock. 'I never thought to take to a stick before I was ninety,' she said, and there was a shrewd glint in her eye as she looked at Joanna. 'You seemed apprehensive as I came in just now – were you expecting to find me a crusty old thing who likes giving orders?'

'I was afraid you wouldn't like me, Miss Corraine.'

'Oh, and why not?'

'Your nephew thinks I shall make a hash of working here.'

'Vance thinks that? I received the impression that he was rather pleased with the arrangement.'

'I meant your nephew Adam—'

'Ah, Adam!' Charlotte Corraine looked quizzical. 'So he was at the airstrip to meet you. What did he have to say?'

Joanna gave an account of the meeting and though she tried to speak as calmly as possible, she couldn't keep a note of indignation out of her voice. 'I believe he thinks I've come here for a holiday!'

'Tough, open-air men are often of the opinion that unless a woman has brawn she is unfit for anything but a life of idleness.' Charlotte spoke drily. 'It's of little use telling them that a reed will bend in a storm, while a tree will often fall. They have to learn for themselves. I need someone reliable to assist me at Raintree, especially since this pesky accident to my foot, and I sensed that you were from your letters. I like also the spirit of adventure that brought you to Australia.

'No, child,' Charlotte shook her head at Joanna, 'don't tell me you came just for the sake of your sister. You came seeking a new way of life, just as I did many years ago. Though Adam and Vance have always called me their aunt, I was Kingsley Corraine's cousin and through him I became the correspondent of his best friend out here in Queensland. I received a proposal of marriage by letter, and though you might not think it a very romantic way to fall in love, Logan and I were in love. He was killed in a cattle-stampede the day I arrived at Wandaday, where he was the manager for Kingsley. I stayed on, to become housekeeper for King when his wife died.'

Charlotte smoothed the curving handle of her stick and a ruby ring gleamed darkly against her brown and weathered hand. An old-fashioned ring, embedded in the third finger of Charlotte's left hand. The ring that had been sent to her years ago by the lover she had never seen –

except perhaps in a photograph.

'I'm sorry,' Joanna murmured. 'It must have been a great shock for you, losing your fiancé in that way.'

'I never lost Logan, my child. When you love someone, the one person you were meant for, he lives on while you live yourself. He is part of you. I met Logan in my dreams if not in reality. I knew exactly how he looked, and dreams don't die as you grow older, they grow stronger, just as memories do.'

There was silence for a moment in the room, while outside in the trees the galahs chattered away. Then Charlotte gave a dry little chuckle. 'I haven't talked like this for years. I suppose because there was no one to really listen. The boys have their work and Bonney would laugh at an old lady's memories.'

'I understand from Mr. Corraine that I am to provide a little companionship for his ward?' Joanna was now feeling much more relaxed; she could even mention the Boss without that betraying shake of angry distress in her voice. No one had ever looked at her as he had done, as if she were a fair scrounger Vance had brought here for his amusement.

'Well, yes, Adam has some sort of idea that she needs female company,' Charlotte said with a slight frown.

'Vance said she was pretty.'

'She's unsettled, Joanna. Doesn't know what she does want, and talks a lot of nonsense about wanting to be a ballet dancer one day, and a nurse the next. Nurse indeed! She nearly passed out when I had my fall and broke this bone in my foot. Adam chivvied me for trying to do too much, but you can't rely on the kitchen help. You have to be behind those girls every minute or they forget to put the yeast in the bread and the tea in the pot. Adam said advertise for a strong young wench and make sure she's used to being miles from a town. Tell her we haven't got television, a dance hall or a cinema, only a barn house where the latest dance is still the foxtrot.'

Charlotte smiled in her dry way at Joanna. 'How long does Adam reckon you'll survive without those amenities?'

'He's given me a fortnight. In that time, Miss Corraine, I've got to prove I can be of use here. If I fail to come up to his expectations then he's packing me off to Hawk's Bay, where he thinks I belong in a boutique! He doesn't spare his punches, does he?'

'He never did, even as a boy. Kingsley was tough with him, because the Boss of a station as big as this one has to be a strong pivot around which everything revolves with ease and industry. With a strong man you know where you are. He can come up with the answers when everyone else is stumped. He can bear the burdens. Of course, to be that way takes toll of whatever charm lies under the armour, but Vance has enough charm for the two of them ... as I am sure you have discovered for yourself, Joanna.'

'He was very kind to me at Hawk's Bay and he made the flight a most interesting one. So many stars.' Joanna smiled. 'I could have reached out of the cockpit of the plane and stolen one.'

'Who else but a born charmer would give a girl a ride among the stars?' Charlotte chuckled. 'I don't think Adam would think of anything so romantic.'

'I am sure he wouldn't!' Joanna bit her lip. 'He'd be more likely to ask one to take a stroll among the stinging trees.'

'But among the stinging trees, my dear, orchids sometimes grow.'

Joanna gazed wide-eyed at Miss Corraine, and it was a

relief when the door swung open and Vance entered carrying a loaded tray. There was a delicious smell of bacon and eggs and toast, and Joanna realized that she was ravenous. She and Vance sat down at a table to eat, while Charlotte Corraine sat watching them over the rim of a teacup. There was in her eyes a look of lively interest.

'You see,' Vance smiled at Joanna, 'you had no need to be scared of Aunt Charly. She has a heart of pure gold.'

'Vance,' murmured his aunt, 'do you mean half the things you say so unblushingly?'

He grinned across at Charlotte. 'I brought you back a lively lobster from the bay. He's out in the jeep in a basket. Bought perfume for the kid, which should take the sulky look off her face for half an hour.'

'She's restless, Vance. At an age when she's torn between acting like a child, and trying her wings as a woman.'

'She's such a little madam at times that I'd tan her bottom if I were Adam.' Vance spoke with an unusual edge to his voice. 'It amazes me, Aunt Charly. With that Bonney baby he's as patient as if gentling a brumbie. Do you reckon he has a father complex about her?'

'He was a great friend of the Ryans, and it was a terrible shock for Bonney, losing both of them at one go.' Charlotte's gaze settled on Joanna, who sat listening to the conversation with the intentness of great interest. 'It was good of Adam, strong of him, to take on the task of telling Bonney her parents had died together in the flood. Lots of men shirk that kind of duty. Reminds me of King when he had to tell me—'

There Charlotte broke off and clutching her cane she heaved herself to her feet. 'I'd better check on Tilly and those onions, then I'll show you to your room, Joanna.'

'You're kind, Miss Corraine.' Joanna spoke sincerely, for she had taken an immense liking to the woman who had cared all her life for other people's children. King's son, and then his grandsons.

'You must call me Aunt Charly like everyone else,' she told Joanna. 'We're one big family at Raintree.'

She was gone, the sound of her cane dying away down the passage that led through the house to the kitchen. 'Salt of the earth,' said Vance. 'She's clung for years to the memory of one man, but no woman with natural instincts should do such a wasteful thing.'

'I don't think Aunt Charly has wasted her life – not entirely,' Joanna said softly. 'She has helped to make Raintree the place it is, and she can't help but feel proud of being part of its backbone. She may have no sons of her own, but she has you, and your cousin.'

'I thought you disliked him?' The corners of Vance's mouth were bent in a grin and his eyes were fixed on her face.

'I'm not saying I like him,' she rejoined. 'It isn't in human nature to like what stings us, but he is obviously a resourceful and keen-minded boss and I expect he will fulfil all his grandfather's hopes in him.'

'And what of me?' Vance asked mockingly. He held a hand across the table, palm upwards, strong and brown and calloused from years of gripping the reins of a horse and riding the range that was so richly stocked with Corraine cattle. 'What do you see in my palm, a long life and a merry one?'

She smiled, for his lifeline was a long one, stretching across the hand she avoided touching. She was a little afraid of what her reaction would be if she allowed her hand to be enfolded by his.

'You will live to be eighty and your family will be a

47

large one,' she said with a laugh.

'You don't think I'll stay a bachelor, Joanna?'

'No man who goes around tossing proposals at girls – as if they were popcorn – is likely to remain a bachelor.'

'Wouldn't you like to marry a Corraine, Miss Darling?'

'Not right now.' And being a girl who couldn't bear to see unwashed dishes on a table, she jumped to her feet, stacked the tray and asked Vance to show her the way to the kitchen.

'You're not going to wash up?' he groaned.

'That's exactly what I am going to do, Mr. Corraine. Now lead the way, please.'

'And I called you a romantic girl,' he said as he held open the door and she whisked past him carrying the loaded tray.

'There's a time and a place for everything,' she said.

'Is that a promise, Joanna?'

She smiled without answering him.

CHAPTER THREE

THE days that followed were filled with new things for Joanna to learn, so many of them that the hours passed like a flash. The meals eaten by the stockriders were large ones, and besides Tilly and Peg, the two aborigine girls who worked in the kitchen, there was Bushy, whose lower left arm was missing. He was sometimes more hindrance than help, but so full of yarns about the bush that Joanna welcomed his weathered face across the tables as they plucked fowls for dinner, or took the stones out of the raisins for a giant plum duff.

As Joanna worked around the enormous kitchen, with its cedar timbering, screened windows to keep out insects, two big stoves and walk-in refrigerator, she absorbed the new sounds in her life. The jingling of spurs, the lowing of the cattle that arose on the warm wind, the laugh of a kookaburra on the branch of a red-gum tree. These trees screened the kitchen from the sun, satiny-patched where the bark had peeled. The scent of peppermint stole in from the gum trees, and there was a droning of bees in the blossoms.

As she sliced fruit into a big blue bowl, or spooned gravy over a great baron of beef, Bushy would softly play the mouth organ he kept in a pocket of his faded check shirt. 'There's peace here, missy,' he aid to her. 'A person can feel the passing of time without having it run away from him.'

But for Joanna those first ten days at Raintree went too fast for any savouring of that peace. She worked away like a little Trojan, though Aunt Charly kept telling her that the boys didn't expect any miracles and didn't mind waiting a few minutes for their meals.

But Adam Corraine expected miracles and Joanna was conscious all the time that she was on trial.

Maybe that was why she burnt a batch of loaves – she who had never done such a thing in her life. Why she upset a large tin of treacle, threw out some forks with the garbage, and cut the runner beans far too thin for the hearty-eating stockriders.

By some miracle of perseverance and green fingers Aunt Charly had cultivated a garden that kept the homestead well supplied with fresh vegetables. It was Bushy's main job to keep the garden watered and free from the weeds that would strangle or smother the homely cabbages, potatoes, onions, marrows and beans.

Joanna delighted in the garden. It was wonderful to see the plump green cabbages growing here in the wilds of Queensland, and she took a snap of the garden to send to Gran, much to the amusement of Bushy, whose offer to appear in the snap was smartly turned down. 'Gran would think I was living among bushrangers,' she said.

'Your folks wanted you to stay home and not go a-roving, is that it, missy?'

'It did surprise my grandmother when I made up my mind to come to Australia, but we both thought I'd be living with my sister, who when I arrived had gone off to New Zealand to appear in a stage show.'

'I had a daughter a long time ago, missy.' Bushy frowned at his harmonica and polished it on his pinned sleeve. 'Trudi she was called. Smart little thing. Her mother took her off to Melbourne and after that I didn't get to see her more than a couple of times. She's married now. Her husband works for the television network and old Bushy Cloud wouldn't be welcome in their posh parlour.'

'Haven't you paid her a visit since she got married, Bushy?'

'Nope. Old Bushy knows where he's welcome, and that's right here, missy. Right here at Raintree. That Adam he's good to me, kept me on when I got poisoning and the doctor came in his plane and took me to Alice Springs to operate on me in that smart hospital they've got there. The Boss didn't pension me off. He knows a man needs to work or he gets like some old dog that lays down in a shady corner one day and dies quietly all by himself. Folks say Adam is like his grandfer, but it ain't rightly so.'

'What do you mean, Bushy?' Joanna turned from her task of shaking down plums for the big tarts the boys liked, served with custard. 'Everyone says he's King all over again – look at that portrait in the drawing-room!'

'Aye, he looks like the old man, and knows how to boss the stockmen and mix with them, but King Corraine was hard all the way through, missy. He never took into account a man's feelings, only his muscles and his ability in the saddle, among them cows. He was so ambitious that he gave off sparks, like a magneto. Some of the aborigine boys called him Willy-Willy, which means a whirlwind.'

Joanna couldn't help but smile, for Adam Corraine was one of the most headlong riders she had ever seen. And if someone dithered about what ought to be done to a broken-down truck, he slid underneath without another word, put the matter right with the all-round skill of a station boss, and emerged looking like a coalminer.

Once or twice he had come into the kitchen looking

like that, and under the tap would go his head and the water would run down his brown neck and plaster his shirt to the shoulders that made Joanna shiver with a girl's fear of the primitive. She felt sure these sallies into the kitchen were made with the intention of watching her at work. As he flicked the water out of his eyes and looked at her, his gaze felt like a lightning in the rain.

The cool grey sparkle of his eyes remained in her thoughts after he had left. He didn't speak to her very much, but she knew he was biding his time, waiting for the end of her trial fortnight to pronounce his verdict. If he sent her away it would be unjust of him. Apart from the upset treacle, the burnt bread, and a few broken plates, she had surely proved that she was a willing worker.

It would be unkind of him, because you couldn't be at Raintree and not find it stealing your heart. Her heart felt stolen – curiously so – but she kept this to herself and didn't even admit to Aunt Charly that it was sheer joy to have a room at the back of the homestead, which overlooked the mystery and magic of the deep valley.

She awoke each morning to bird song, and to the sunshot mist that slowly unveiled the trees. The dew turned to perfume on the flowering creepers, and there was a jewelled flash of wings as the tiny bush birds flew from branch to branch. Joanna was used to being up and about at an early hour, and by the time she and the two girls started the steak and onions for the boys, she had fed the hens, milked the few domestic cows, and had time to smile at the trio of comical kookaburras perched on a branch like chatter-happy ladies all got up in their best feathers for an outing.

She had no time in those first two weeks to get really acquainted with Bonney Ryan, who steered clear of the kitchen and seemed to spend a lot of her time mooning over poetry, or playing the records of a certain pop hero with a fantastic name. She had a Celtic prettiness that was somewhat marred by a petulant mouth. Her dark hair was smooth as silk, and her eyes were the brown of a highland tarn. Joanna could understand why Adam Corraine didn't like her riding alone. She was at the romantic age, and several of the stockmen were young and unmarried, and they had about them a brown-skinned, dashing attractiveness as they rode off on their horses, a stockwhip coiled around a broad shoulder.

Several invitations to the next barn dance had already come Joanna's way, but she could make no promises. The barn dance was on Saturday, and by then she might have been packed off to Hawk's Bay, found wanting by the Boss, who had looked at her so coldly that first day and whose ice had not melted beyond a cool: 'Good morning, Miss Dowling. Please remember that I like my eggs sunny side down.'

One evening at sundown Joanna found herself alone on the veranda that overlooked the valley. She had showered and slipped into a cool sleeveless dress, and she leaned against the veranda post and savoured the wonderful stillness as the sun faded into a violet dusk. There was a seductive scent of honeysuckle from the great cluster over the trellis, and the afterglow seemed to cling round the mountains like a halo.

For the first time she felt a sense of peace, and then it was broken as a voice spoke behind her on the veranda. 'Taking a breather from your chores, Miss Dowling?'

She swung round and there was Adam Corraine, a tall figure in the dusk, the light of a match playing over his face as he lit his pipe. The tang of the tobacco floated to her, mingling with the sweet honeysuckle, and the quickened beat of her heart told her that the moment had come for them to discuss her future.

'Strange how the coming of night changes the look of things, eh?' His tread was deep on the boards of the veranda as he came to stand nearby. 'You must find Australia very different from England?'

'It's all rather overwhelming,' she agreed, 'but I'm doing my best to cope. I suppose you want to talk about that, Mr. Corraine? I am aware that my fortnight is up – almost.'

'Having someone here has certainly taken a load off my aunt's shoulders, but there are aspects to living as we do, miles from our nearest neighbours and the bustle of a town, that might in another couple of weeks make you wish you had never set eyes on Raintree. Australian girls are used to the life—'

'You can only get used to a place by living in it,' she argued. 'It's like people. How can one tell from appearance what a person is really like? Shyness can hide aggression. Brusqueness can be a mask for reserve.'

'It's rare for a home-help to be a student of philosophy,' he drawled.

'It's mere good sense, Mr. Corraine, to know that the sweetness of an apple can't be assured unless one takes a bite.'

He drew on his pipe and his soft laugh was enigmatical. He might have been amused by her reasoning, but she felt that if she looked into his eyes she would see a mocking light in them. It was as if there was no ground they could meet on without this sense of tension and battle. She looked away from him, but was very aware of his considerable tallness, even lounging against the veranda rail.

'You've taken but a nibble of the apple,' he said. 'What about later on when it gets really hot, when everything is

54

quiet with Vance and the boys away mustering? A large apple is not firm and sweet all round. There might be patches that could set your small white teeth on edge.'

'You – you talk as if I'm a child!' It both confused her and annoyed her that he should mention anything personal about her. Her teeth were quite nice, but they weren't *milk* teeth. 'I don't expect everything to be tame and cosy here at Raintree. I'm well aware that it isn't a holiday resort!'

'Some women would think it a hardship to be miles from the fancy shops and the hairdressing salon; lush restaurants and theatres.'

'Mr. Corraine, if you were talking to my sister Viviana, then all this would be relevant. She is the Dowling girl who likes to be within reach of smart shops and theatres, not I. I find the countryside peaceful, not monotonous.'

'Fighting words, Miss Dowling.' His eyes flicked her hair, her winged eyebrows, her mouth that held a young and touching obstinacy. The stars came out beyond his shoulder and from the men's quarters came the sound of guitar music. 'There are people who take root here like the brigalow tree, but let's you and me be honest. Isn't it because of my cousin that you're so keen to stay here?'

For a stunned moment she could hardly believe her ears. There was a tense silence filled with the faint sound of music, and her eyes matched the spark of the fireflies. 'If you want the truth, then here it is,' she said frostily. 'I don't like cities and was prepared to put up with your rudeness in order to work in a beautiful place like this valley. I don't have to put up with cooking for a crowd of stockmen. I could cook for just one man if I wished—'

'Meaning?' Adam Corraine's voice had gone softly dangerous, in contrast to the sudden sweet call of a bush bird.

'Your cousin asked me to marry him,' she said recklessly. 'I know you don't want me at Raintree, but if I marry Vance then you'll have to put up with me!'

She stood taut against the cloud of honeysuckle, wanting to bury herself in it a second after her crazy statement. To a man like Adam Corraine marriage would be a serious proposition. He wouldn't jest about it, as she knew Vance had been jesting. Her heart hammered. What would he do? She watched silently as he tapped the ashes from his pipe, a tall, spare man, with a profile marred by the broken bridge of a dominant nose. A man contained within himself, as the valley was, and the mountains. She trembled a little and wished she had the courage and poise to laugh off what she had just said about Vance wanting to marry her.

Then Adam turned to look at her. 'You're a fast worker, Miss Dowling. You must have got that proposal out of Vance almost as soon as you met him, seeing as how he's been at Once-Lonely working on that bore for the past couple of weeks.'

'Yes, I was so anxious to be married,' she flared, 'that I've been burning my fingers on those big gas cookers for the past two weeks, loading and unloading great baking tins of potatoes and beef!' She drew away from the veranda rail and went to sweep past him. 'Keep your job, Mr. Corraine. You're too exhausting to please!'

'Just a minute.' His hand caught her elbow in a firm grip. 'If I let you go, that ardent cousin of mine will waste his weekends making visits to Hawk's Bay. You'd better stay here.'

'I wouldn't stay if you gave me another pound a week!' She wrestled with him in an effort to break free of his grip, but the hand that held her was the same one that handled a raking chestnut horse, and it was tiring, not to say undignified, trying to escape his iron fingers. She breathed quickly and was confused at finding herself too close to him. Pine soap and tobacco smoke mingled in her nostrils.

'The job is yours,' he said firmly. 'I like a fighter, though at first glance you don't give that impression. My father fought alongside the English in Burma and he wrote in his letters home that they were "cool as cucumbers, and they don't cry in company". Aunt Charly also tells me that you don't get impatient with her ramblings, or Bushy's. That's unusual in a young person.'

'I was brought up by my grandmother,' Joanna reminded him, somewhat disarmed by what he had said about his father, who had fought and died in the jungles of Burma and left his son to be reared by the autocratic King Corraine.

'I'm fond of my aunt,' he said roughly, as if a revelation of his feelings was more difficult for him than roping a scrub bull or taming a range horse. She was amazed to find herself smiling a little in the shadows where he still held her, his fingers tough and warm about her slender arm. 'I'd do a lot for her.'

'You'd even let me stay at Raintree, though I set your teeth on edge?' The smile still lingered on Joanna's lips, for some reason.

'Now I didn't say that—'

'You said an Australian girl would suit you best, so if you'll release me I'll go in and pack my bag.'

He didn't release her, and as the seconds ticked by and the night sounds from the valley drifted to them, Joanna felt the fight go out of her. She felt a sense of surrender to the place and the master. There was nothing tame about either of them – a mere girl could not withstand their silent strength, their hold on the imagination.

'Now you're forcing me to stay?' she murmured. 'Does it please you better?'

'Pleases both of us,' he retorted. 'Women like to be bossed.'

'Or they do the bossing?'

'Exactly.'

'You're a ruthless man, Mr. Corraine.'

'But my cousin is charming.'

'Yes, he's a born charmer.'

'Something women like even better.'

'Can you blame them?'

'No.'

He let her go and where his hand had held her arm there lingered an impression of strength and rough warmth. She wondered if he minded that his cousin was easier to like, with a grace to him that made Adam seem rugged and a bit fierce. He was like the horse or the bull that led the mob ... you didn't try to get a rope on him because it wasn't in his nature to be roped. He'd trample over anyone who tried, be it a man or a woman.

She gazed from the veranda and thought the trees in the starlight had silver trunks patched with black velvet. 'I like Miss Charlotte,' she said, as if in this moment she needed to let Adam know that it wasn't just for Vance that she stayed. 'I like her very much. I think her life has been selfless and rather wonderful. She must once have been very beautiful.'

'Yes,' he said, in that rough tone. 'But if we've a purpose and it's a good one, and we squander ourselves for it, then I reckon we're living.'

'You think it's better to have a purpose than a love?' Joanna dared to ask. 'It must at times be a bit lonely.'

'It could be lonelier if the love we accept is not the love we really want.'

'Then you believe there is only one soulmate for each of us, Mr. Corraine?'

'Don't you, Miss Dowling?'

Of course, she wanted to say. I believe with all my heart in one true love, but it was an intimate subject and she thought it wise that she remain impersonal in her dealings with the Boss of Raintree. Tomorrow or the next day she might do something an Australian girl wouldn't do, and Adam's frown was easier borne if a girl kept her distance.

'How many different sounds there are at night at Raintree,' she said. 'Have you ever tried to count them?'

'They're part of living and breathing to me.' His voice held distance as he straightened to his full height. 'Shall we go in and join the others for dinner?'

She preceded him, and as they entered the dining-room together, Bonney Ryan glanced round from the window where she was standing and the light was soft on her silky dark hair, but her eyes were sharp as she took in the slender fair figure of Joanna ... startlingly fair against the leathery tan and toughness of Adam Corraine.

'Adam, I wanted to talk to you.' The girl brushed past Joanna and caught at his arm possessively. 'Where have you been?'

'Out on the veranda discussing business with Miss Dowling.' He smiled down at Bonney and his face revealed his affection for the pretty young thing. 'What have you got on your mind, honey?'

Joanna blinked a little, for that endearing term sounded strange on the lips that looked so firm, as if only used to giving orders. She drew away from the couple and stood admiring the flowers in a vase on the table, which was circular and laid for four people. Aunt Charly had insisted from the start that Joanna dine with the family.

59

She felt awkward, however, for she couldn't help but hear what Bonney said to her tall guardian. 'It's about having a little car of my own – Adam, you more or less promised, and I'd love taking lessons from you.'

'You're a bit young yet to drive a car, Bonney.'

'I'm almost eighteen.' Out of the tail of her eye Joanna saw the girl reach up and caress his lean brown cheek. 'Please, Adam. If I had a car I could drive out to the Farlins' place and visit with Mona. We were at school together and I miss my friends.'

'You're welcome to go in the jeep, honey, whenever you want to go and see your friend.'

'It isn't the same, going places in that old jeep with Jim Long driving.' A sulky note came into the girl's voice. 'You aren't going back on your word, are you? You said I could have something special for my eighteenth birthday, and it's only a month away.'

'I had in mind a real little thoroughbred for you, maybe a silver-tailed roan—'

'A horse!' Bonney broke in. 'I already have Satin and she does for riding when I'm in the mood. But I'm not really the equestrian type. My limbs are too delicate.'

Even as Joanna smiled to herself, Adam gave a laugh. 'You look pretty robust to me, Bonney.'

'I'm built like a ballet dancer,' she said indignantly, 'and I won't let my legs get bowed with too much horse-back riding. Suppose I decide to go on the stage?'

'Last week you were thinking about becoming an air hostess.' He glanced over the girl's head at Joanna and there was in his eyes a deep smile that made Joanna think of lakes lit by flashes of sunlight. Striking eyes in that rugged brown face. 'What were you like at seventeen?' he asked. 'Did you want to be a ballet dancer, or nurse to a flying doctor?'

Even as Joanna considered the question, she saw Bonney flick a look of dislike over her. It chilled her, made her realize that she was the outsider at Raintree.

'I was always so enthralled by my twin's ambitions that I had no time for any of my own,' Joanna said with a brave lightness, a wish that she was less sensitive and more like Viviana in her ways. 'My sister went on the stage and she loves the life and has that glow about her that lights her up on the stage.'

'I suppose she's prettier than you?' said Bonney. 'There were twins at my school who weren't a bit alike. Is your sister a chorus dancer?'

'At the moment,' said Joanna, feeling a little like shaking this spoiled young ward of Adam's, 'Viviana is starring in a show in New Zealand.'

'Why didn't you go there instead of coming here?'

Joanna flinched and felt again a bleak sense of loneliness among strangers, and then before she could say that lack of money had stopped her from flying to her sister, the Boss swung Bonney to face him and he looked very stern about the eyes and mouth.

'One of these days, young lady, I shall take Vance's advice and tan your breeches. If you're old enough to drive a car of your own, then you're old enough to be polite to whoever comes under the roof of Raintree.'

'Vance!' Bonney said scornfully. 'He'd like to be the boss here, then he could put *me* in the kitchen to work. He hates me!'

'Don't be silly.' Adam tweaked the girl's hair. 'You'd get along all right with Vance if you didn't argue with him about everything. Most females get along fine with him.'

Bonney gave Joanna a long stare, and it was a relief when Aunt Charly came limping into the room, followed by Tilly and Peg in the spotless aprons they wore for serving dinner each evening. This was a bit of grandeur Aunt Charly liked to lay on for the Boss, along with the candlesticks of old silver and the flowers that made the evening meal such a pleasant one.

After dinner Adam went to his office to talk to someone over the radio-telephone. Bonney followed him, and Joanna caught the way Aunt Charly frowned. 'She's after something again, and Adam gives in to her because of the way she lost her folks. Vance wouldn't be so soft with her.'

Joanna gazed in some surprise at Charlotte.

'Don't let it surprise you that Vance has more sense when it comes to women.' Aunt Charly gave a chuckle as she led Joanna into her snug sitting-room. 'He has a lot less when it comes to business matters – take a chair, child, and tell me, has Adam been sensible with regard to you? Is he satisfied that you'll be good for his beloved Raintree Valley.'

Joanna smiled as she sat back in a cushioned cane chair and let her eyes dwell on the old-fashioned comforts of the room, and the long zinnia-patterned curtains. 'He isn't entirely convinced that I'm right for the job, but he likes the way I get along with Bushy, and with you, Aunt Charly.'

'So he's letting you stay for my sake?'

'Yes, I think so.' Joanna leaned forward to a little table on which stood some framed photographs and she picked up an oval one with a silver surround. It was of a girl in a fur bonnet with a muff held against her. Charming, youthful eyes smiled with happiness, with an expectancy that made her very lovely.

'I had been skating on the lake near our home at Hampstead the day that was taken.' Charlotte spoke nostalgically. 'The little things one remembers. Leaves frozen under the ice, a blackbird calling and hot chestnuts round a charcoal brazier.'

'Do you sometimes wish you had stayed in England?' Joanna asked.

'Do you mean,' Charlotte's still youthful eyes held Joanna's, 'do I wish I'd never let myself fall in love with a faraway stranger?'

'You would probably have married in England and been happy,' Joanna said softly.

'Every girls wants a happy love,' Aunt Charly agreed. 'But she wants something else besides – romance and challenge and colour. She wants to live like a heroine, not like a humdrum keeper of a home, and girls of my generation were no less adventurous than those of today, who seek experience beyond their own shores. Was it the call of your twin, or the call of something more primitive that brought you halfway across the world, Joanna?'

'I ... I don't really know,' Joanna said honestly. 'I never envied Viv her free spirit, but when she invited me to join her I never hesitated for very long. I could see Gran would be all right with her widowed sister, and I was over twenty-one.'

'Did it frighten you when you found yourself all alone in Australia?'

'It alarmed me—'

Aunt Charly gave a chuckle. 'If men really knew how spunky we really are! You were miles from home with only a few pounds in your pocket, but without getting into a dither you found yourself a job. That's what perplexes Adam. You look as soft as wattle—'

'Wattle?' Joanna broke in.

'Our name for mimosa.'

'Oh—'

'Well, mimosa's a pale gold, airy-fairy flower, isn't it?'

'And you think that's how I strike the Boss, as an airy-fairy bit of fluff on a slim stalk?'

Aunt Charly was still laughing when the door opened and Adam strolled into the room. He glanced from the older woman to the much younger one and his right eyebrow formed part of a question mark. 'Is it a joke for sharing with a man?' he drawled, and the room and its old-fashioned knick-knacks seemed suddenly too small to hold so high, wide and free a man.

'It's a joke I'd love to be able to tell you,' laughed Aunt Charly, 'but I don't want to lose Joanna now you've said she can stay to brighten my old age. Where's Bonney?'

'Having a galah session with a girl friend at Danabarra. The things girls find to natter about! Something about a new skin cream, and the latest pop record by some fellow called Engelbert.'

It was Joanna's turn to break into a laugh, which a flash of the sky-grey eyes couldn't stem.

'Girls will be girls,' said Aunt Charly reasonably. 'Now don't prowl, Adam. You'll break one of my porcelains and I set store by them. Sit down, do, and smoke your pipe – if you have to.'

He looked around him, as if for a suitable chair, and Joanna pressed a thumb against her lips and tried to control their quivering. He looked like a stag in a china shop and if he didn't sit down soon something on one of the whatnots would go flying. Their glances met as he lowered himself to a sofa with chintz cushions. Amusement tugged at the left corner of his mouth, and it gave her a tiny shock that he should be sharing her thoughts.

Adam Corraine was not a man for the hearth and the

cushion; he was built for the open country, made to stretch out beside a campfire under the stars. Would he ever marry and take the chance of being domesticated? It was something she couldn't imagine, but Raintree was built to last and he would want a son of his own to take over when the time came.

'Do you ride, Miss Dowling?' he asked suddenly, and she couldn't help but be aware of the flick of his eyes over her ankles and slender legs. Mimosa flitted through her mind, pale gold and fragile.

'As a country child it was something I learned young and liked.' She smiled. 'Your cousin Vance warned me that I would find the bush horse harder to handle.'

'I'm quite sure you would.' Adam tinkered with his pipe but didn't light it, while Aunt Charly sat at ease in her armchair and shared a lazily interested look between Joanna and the Boss. Her plastered ankle was propped on a footrest, her eyes were still a charming blue as they gazed from the network of lines the years and the sun had etched into her once-lovely face. There was no air of regret about Charlotte Corraine, only pride in what she had helped to build.

'We keep several polo ponies in our stables and they're well trained.'

'Polo ponies?' Joanna exclaimed.

'Yes, there's a polo club at Danabarra, and Vance and I play when we aren't busy. We send the ponies by truck, and Aunt Charly and Bonney drive in with us for the game.' A slightly sardonic smile crisped the edge of his mouth. 'There's a small hotel, a bank, a store, and the club. To an outsider the place might seem rugged, but we like it. It's the nearest thing we have to civilization.'

Joanna shot a smile at Aunt Charly. 'Mr. Corraine has got it into his head that I'll find it hard to settle down so many miles from a beauty salon or a teashop. I told him it's my twin who is the gay and lively one.'

'I think you've plenty of life in you, Joanna. You flit round that big kitchen of ours like a summer bee. It's very pleasant, Adam. Our shy Joanna sings when she thinks no one is listening.'

'You're making her blush,' Adam drawled.

You're the one, Joanna wanted to protest. *You with those grey eyes that don't miss a thing.*

'Is there any particular pony that I may ride, Mr. Corraine?'

'Brindle should suit you. He has a friendly nature, and it will be good for Bonney to have a riding companion. Do you like my ward, Miss Dowling?'

'She's extremely pretty.'

'Yes,' he looked thoughtful, 'she has grown into a pretty thing.'

'You're spoiling her, Adam,' warned Aunt Charly. 'She's learning fast what a big pair of eyes can do to a man, and if you're not careful you'll have trouble on your hands.'

'You mean with one of the boys?'

'Well, if you've noticed that she's pretty!'

'You talk, Aunt Charly, as if I go around with my eyes shut.'

'On the contrary, Adam. Anyone can see that you have twenty-twenty vision, but you are inclined to devote most of it to cows, machines, and grazing land.'

'Meaning I don't always see what is under my nose?' He frowned and looked rather arrogant. 'The stockmen know me, and they know I won't tolerate any pranks involving Bonney. She's not more than a child.'

'She's almost eighteen. Your own mother was a bride at that age.'

66

His frown deepened. 'Are you suggesting I find a husband for Bonney?'

'I'm saying that she has too much time on her hands, and you know the old saying about the devil and the idle.'

'You mean it might be a good idea to let her go and work as a nurse?'

'Nurse my foot!' Aunt Charly almost snorted. 'Tell her to help out more, here at Raintree. She could assist Joanna and learn how to cook and make a good pot of tea. It's your place, Adam, to let her know that we all do our bit here, and that acting the princess isn't good training for any girl who hopes to land her man.'

'Her man?' Adam quirked an eyebrow. 'I suppose you know who the fellow happens to be?'

'I have my suspicions.'

'But you're not sharing them?'

'Romantic old maids revel in secrets, Adam.'

'An old maid, you?' He rose to his feet, leaned over Aunt Charly and kissed her temple beneath the grey hair that held gleams of auburn, as if always youth would linger in this woman who had lost the man she had wanted but who had not turned bitter. Instead she had served and loved the Corraines, and right now she touched the hard brown cheek of Adam Corraine as if in him she saw the realization of long-held dreams.

Aunt Charly would want this strong and able master of Raintree to take a wife ... was it possible, Joanna wondered, that she had Bonney in mind for him?

Bonney, with her big tarn-brown eyes and her way of snuggling beneath the wide spread of Adam's shoulders. He was indulgent with the pretty thing ... maybe as yet she had not sparked the fires in that powerful frame, but Aunt Charly was wise. She had hinted that Bonney cared

67

for someone, and Adam had looked arrogant, as if no man but he would have the love of pretty Bonney Ryan.

Saturday morning came with a blue sky pebbled with gold, and there were singing birds in the blue gum trees.

Today Vance was due home from Once-Lonely, and tonight there would be dancing in the barn-hall with its long corrugated iron roof and its shining cedarwood floor, laid long ago by order of King Corraine. Meetings and discussions took place in the barn-hall, including the ladies' club organized and run by Charlotte.

Joanna knew herself to be a source of curiosity to the valley wives, for not only was she English but she was single, and they'd be watching closely at the dance to see which bachelor stockrider she favoured. She must favour none ... Vance least of all! He was a Corraine and it wouldn't do to give rise to speculation by dancing more with him than with some of the other boys.

She smiled and with floury hands she walked to the open door of the big kitchen and gazed out at the vegetable garden bordered by golden buttercup trees. She looked forward to seeing Vance, and hoped he had missed her a little. Tall, sun-brown Vance, with a subtle resemblance to his cousin Adam that you saw one minute and missed the next. She found her thoughts fixed for a brief moment on Adam. Would he attend the dance? As Boss of the community he would no doubt put in an appearance, but Joanna couldn't picture him on the dance floor. He was far more at home in the saddle of Blaze, his chestnut with the raking lines and the one blaze of white on the forehead beneath the wild sweeping mane.

Suddenly through the garden there came a young woman in a full blue skirt and a lacy peasant-type blouse.

She carried a basket on her arm and wore a linen sunhat. Her eyes sparkled darkly as she came with grace down the path between the cabbages and potatoes.

'*Buon giorno, signorina.*' White teeth flashed in a friendly smile. 'I am Lenita, the wife of Boye Dawson, and I thought it time we introduced ourselves. I come from Italy before I marry Boye, and always we bring some small thing with which to greet a newcomer.'

With a charming gesture the girl held out the basket and there surrounded by green leaves was a pot of basil. Nurtured, tended, and growing far from Italy. Joanna wiped her hands quickly on her apron and took the pot. She smelled the basil and felt the sting of tears behind her eyelids. 'How kind of you,' she said huskily. 'Nothing could please me more.'

'May the basil grow as our friendship grows.' Lenita's eyes were frank and appealing as they dwelt on Joanna. 'I thought from seeing you that first day that you would be nice to know. I have wanted to come and greet you, but Boye said I must wait in case you went away again.'

'Did everyone think I would go away?' Joanna's smile was wry.

'Boye was told by the other men that Signor Corraine looked staggered when he saw you by the monoplane. They thought,' Lenita gave a breathless little laugh, 'that he would bundle you back on the plane and order Vance to fetch someone bigger and stronger for the home-helping.'

'I had come all the way from Sydney and he wasn't getting rid of me as easily as that.' Joanna caressed the smooth sides of the pot of basil. 'I've wanted to come and see your baby – may I come, Lenita, now the Boss has accepted me as part of the Raintree Valley community?'

'But of course,' Lenita looked delighted. 'I should be so pleased for you to come and admire my little Carlo. Such a baby! He grows so big and Boye is so proud of him. A man likes so much to have a son, and I shall always remember the look on my husband's face when he saw Carlo for the first time. Such a smile! As if he held the world in his arms.'

At these words a little chill of emotion ran over Joanna, but for the life of her she didn't know why a sudden vision of Adam Corraine should float into her mind. She neither cared, nor was she involved in that intimate aspect of his future, and she said quickly to Lenita: 'I've been baking treacle tarts. Aunt Charly and the two girls, along with Bushy, are over at the barn-hall hanging bunting for the dance tonight.'

'You are looking forward to the dance?' Lenita smiled with the happy confidence of a girl who had found her man and was delightfully happy with him.

'Yes, it will make a nice break. Come in, Lenita, and I'll give you a cup of tea. Or would you prefer coffee?'

'Coffee, please.' The Italian girl followed Joanna into the kitchen, where she took off her sunhat and revealed the glossy darkness of her hair. She was quite lovely, and Joanna felt again that she must be rather plain in comparison to these girls at Raintree Valley. She invited Lenita to take a chair, and had no idea as she set about making the coffee that the flush in her cheeks and the wayward lock of hair above her smoke-blue eyes made her appealing in a very English way. She felt Lenita watching her with dark, interested eyes.

'How long have you been in Australia?' she asked the Italian girl.

'I came here with my brother and his wife about five years ago. They have a small restaurant in Sydney, near the Opera House. I worked for them, and met Boye when he was there on holiday.' Lenita lowered her eyes and her lashes looked very long and curly. 'We knew at once that we cared. Just a look and we knew. It is sometimes like that, and we married quickly and he brought me home with him to the valley. One remembers Italy, with the lime trees alive with birds, and the vineyards, but I would be happy anywhere with Boye. We have a nice home, and Signor Corraine is a good man to work for.'

Joanna set a cup of coffee and a slice of cake in front of Lenita and sat down to relax with her own cup of coffee. 'He certainly has plenty of drive and ambition, and I can tell from the little I've so far seen of the station that it must be one of the best in Queensland. Up to date, clean and thriving, and yet somehow unspoiled. It would take a keen and imaginative man to achieve all that.'

Lenita caught Joanna's gaze over the rim of her coffee cup. 'I think you are not quite sure of him as a person, *signorina*.'

'Please call me Joanna! We English are always a little cautious when it comes to our feelings about other people.'

'You are not impulsive like an Italian, eh?'

Joanna smiled. 'Impulsive in action, very often, but we're basically shy in our human contacts. The armour of the Crusaders and the restrictions of the Puritans have left their mark. To fall in love on sight would be something we might fight.'

'Ah, but love is the best thing of all in life. It must not be something to run away from, Joanna.'

'Not if it's mutual,' Joanna agreed. 'But it would be awful to give away your love to someone who didn't want it. We English buckle on our armour just in case.'

'Is it not uncomfortable?' A deep dimple showed in

Lenita's cheek.

'Much more uncomfortable to give yourself away to someone who hasn't really noticed that you're alive.'

'Supposing the man thinks that as well, then there are the two of you, clanking about in your uncomfortable armour when all you really want is to be in each other's arms.'

Joanna laughed outright and felt the quick birth of affection for this Latin girl, who like herself had come from a far country to seek a new life, a fresh bounty of experiences in Australia.

'When may I come to see Carlo?' she asked.

'Whenever you are free. Our bungalow is the one with the blue shutters and the cream walls, and the little swing between the poinciana trees on the lawn.'

After Lenita had left, Joanna cradled the little pot of basil and heard in the quiet the flying chuckle of a bower bird. 'Our bungalow,' the words lingered. 'The one with the blue shutters.'

CHAPTER FOUR

THE sun went to topaz and the west was aflame with rose and tinges of violet. Tiny rosellas flew to their perches in the trees, and a hawk was etched with outspread wings against the glowing sky. The going down of the sun seemed to fill the valley with a beauty beyond words, and then a galah let out a squawk and the trees turned to tall dark shadows.

The air was cool now; a moment more and the sun had smouldered away and the valley was quiet.

Joanna, dressed and ready for the dance, walked down by the paddock fence, where some young horses, brought in for gentling, stood like statues in the afterglow. One of them whinnied and thrust his head over the rail. Joanna put out a hand and felt the warm breath against her fingers, then the thrust of velvet nostrils. She smiled a little. So bush horses were too tough for her to handle, eh?

Then all at once the colts became restless. Ears pricked and the one with the soft nose galloped off across the paddock. Joanna listened and heard plainly the sound of galloping hooves coming up the rise towards the house. She turned and watched and as the rider came into view he saluted with his whip and his horse cleared the gate and she heard the ring of a familiar laugh.

'Is that you, Joanna?' He vaulted from the saddle. 'I've come to take you dancing.'

She felt a rush of pleasure, such as a stranger feels when she sees a friend. She felt herself gripped by warm, rough, cattleman hands, and as she she lifted her face to Vance he bent and had kissed her lips before she could stop him.

'Oh—' she said. 'Show-off!'

'Have you missed me, Miss Darling?' He gave his throaty laugh.

'I've been far too busy.' It was good to see him again, with his gay, audacious eyes, and his charm that made him so easy to be with.

'Little teaser.' His hand travelled from her shoulder to her waist, caressingly. 'All dressed up for the barn dance, eh? Mmm, nice material.'

She was very slim of figure in her magnolia-white dress with a pattern of soft green leaves, but when she tried to draw away from Vance his fingers tightened against her waist and he compelled her to stay close. 'Bashful?' he mocked.

She looked up at him and the new young moon was in her eyes. 'No, I just don't want to arrive at the dance looking – kissed.'

'Don't let's go to the dance.' He gestured at the moon. 'It's a young one riding over the valley, and there's a bridge to the rain forest, just made for a kissing couple.'

'We're not that, Vance!' Again in a panic, because he charmed her, she tried to pull away from him. They were struggling a little, and he was laughing, when a tall figure came striding past from the direction of the house. He tipped his slouch hat.

'Hullo, Vance! You must tell me how things went at Once-Lonely – when you're not quite so busy.'

The tall figure strode on, pushing open the side gate and letting it clang shut behind him. His face in the moonlight had been hard and unrevealing, but Joanna was quite sure that he hadn't missed a detail of her white-clad figure pressed forcibly against Vance.

'Now look what you've done!' she pulled away from his slackened hands. 'Your cousin won't like you flirting with the home-help.'

'Adam can't stop me if I flirt out of working hours,' Vance grinned. 'We haven't all been blessed with his brand of self-control. He's a born bachelor who will have to take a bride ... or see Raintree go to a son of mine.'

Joanna's hand shook a little as she smoothed her hair. 'Let's be on our way to the dance ...'

'Joanna,' Vance's voice was a whisper against her ear, 'you entice like a cool willow at the end of a hot day. For two days I've been travelling home to you, and I couldn't care a snap of the fingers if Adam saw me holding you. It would do him good to hold a girl more often ... tell me something, does it intrigue a girl when she comes up against a rugged individual like my cousin?'

'What exactly do you mean?' Her eyes dwelt wide and wondering on Vance, and she saw the corners of his mouth bend in a quizzical smile.

'Wouldn't you like to shake him out of his armour?'

'No indeed!'

'Why not, Joanna? Do you think he'd be dangerous if a girl sparked off the slow-burning fires in that man of iron?'

'Mr. Corraine is my employer,' she said firmly. 'I don't know what he'd be like "sparked off" as you put it, and I don't wish to know.'

'Come off it, Joanna. There isn't a single woman for two hundred miles who wouldn't like to get under the guard of the Boss of Raintree. He's a challenge to women as an obstinate scrub stallion is to a stockman. He won't be caught and they'd like nothing better than to see someone bring him to his knees.'

'You speak as if you don't really like him,' Joanna said,

and she found the fact disquieting. It seemed like a flaw in Vance that he could resent Adam. 'Would you like to see him brought to his knees?'

Vance gazed over towards the mountains, dark shapes above the valley, and he shook his head. 'I guess he needles me at times because he's what I could never be, a man with a single purpose. But I'm not really sure that it's right for a man to be that way. Somehow it rules out a warm, crazy love for a woman, and I don't think I could live without that. Like King he'll always put business first ... they always say that King's wife died of being lonely for a man who always looked beyond her to Raintree.'

'Bushy says that Adam isn't entirely like his grandfather. The old swaggy reckons he cares more for people than King Corraine ever did.'

'Maybe ... a little.' Vance flicked a look over her moonlit heart of a face, with the fair hair drawn back in its usual neat style. 'Are you defending him, Joanna?'

'Well, I know what it feels like to be misjudged.'

'It was Adam who judged you for a girl who couldn't push for herself.'

'You've just said, Vance, that he spends all his time planning for the stations. I expect he can judge good beef at a single glance.'

Vance let out a laugh. 'That's what I've missed as well, that flash of unexpected fun in you, Joanna Darling.'

'Watch your accent, Mr. Corraine!'

His laugh deepened and he touched a hand to her hair. 'Let it loose, Joanna. Be a devil.'

'No ...' She backed away from him. 'I can hear the music drifting up from the barn-hall. The dancing has started, Vance. We'll be late.'

'We'll go to the ball on my knightly charger.' His teeth flashed as he gestured at his horse, Rebellion, a handsome grey whose coat shone like mail in the moonlight. He vaulted into the saddle, then directed Joanna to step on his stirruped foot, to take his hand and let herself be lifted in front of him. His arm curved around her, and the grey broke into a gallop that carried them down the hill, through the soft wind and the moonlight, towards the barn-hall where the long veranda was lit by coloured lanterns, and where a barbecue was set up on the lawn of buffalo grass.

It was a gay spectacle, the glow of the lanterns against the honey-stoned walls of the barn, with a great swathe of scented trumpet flower tumbling from the roof. The sound of dancing mingled with the record music and the happy laughter.

'Here we are, Cinderella.' Vance brought his horse to a standstill and she slid to the ground. She stood in confusion a minute, aware of the men on the veranda, watching with grins over their tankards of beer.

'I guess that job at Once-Lonely was a bore in more ways than one,' a stockman called out. 'You look pleased to be home, Vance.'

Vance secured the bridle of his horse to a rail and as Joanna preceded him up the steps towards the group of men, she realized that she had been optimistic in hoping she could avoid notice by dancing with the other bachelors. Even as they asked for a dance, Vance took her by the elbow and said possessively that she was all booked up.

'My bonus for having to do that job at Once-Lonely,' he drawled. 'You boys have had over a week to stake your claims.'

'The young lady wasn't sure—'

'That she'd be staying?' Vance swept off his slouch hat and his brown hair sprang in a wave above his audacious eyes. 'You can scotch the rumour as from now. Miss Dowling is staying. The Boss says so.'

'Good-o!' It was one of the younger men who spoke. His name was Tye and the other day he had come to Joanna with a cut arm. He was a pearl-diver turned drover, and while Joanna had applied antiseptic and bandaged him, he had told her about some of his exploits, how on one occasion he had dived too deep and come dangerously close to getting the bends, which could cripple a man. She liked Tye and gave him a smile over her shoulder. He winked and she knew he'd get a dance with her before the evening was out.

The hall was brightly lit and gay with bunting, spiky red flowers, and the casual but colourful dresses of the women. The older women sat about in comfortable chairs with wicker sides, and even as Aunt Charly gave a wave and the dance music started up again, Joanna felt as if lightning struck as a grey glance met hers across the room of dancing couples. She stumbled and Vance tightened his arm about her. She looked away as casually as possible from Adam, but still in her mind's eye she could see him. She was deeply shaken by his look of distinction in a tropical worsted suit and a white shirt whose collar was pristine against the brown of his throat.

She couldn't help but give him another cautious glance, and this time he was dancing with Bonney. The Boss's ward was rather more than pretty tonight. There was a pale starry flower in her dark hair, and her dress was the colour of a wild geranium. She danced close to Adam and her eyes shone with the pleasure of a conquest.

'Wonders will never cease,' Vance murmured in Joanna's ear. 'The Boss usually puts in an appearance at these barn parties, but he doesn't often dance at them.'

'Bonney looks irresistible,' Joanna smiled. 'He's terribly fond of her . . . anyone can see it.'

'You think so?' Vance followed the other couple with his eyes. 'Yes, she's looking quite the little lady tonight . . . and proud of herself for having the Boss in tow.' He inclined his head as they danced past his cousin and Bonney. 'Hullo, kid. You're almost the belle of the ball tonight.'

Bonney tossed her head and gave Joanna a stare. It was a look that took in the English girl's fairness of hair and skin, and the quiet charm of her white dress with its pattern of leaves. Joanna felt herself tensing in Vance's arms, and then the music changed its rhythm and it was a relief to find herself in the midst of a rollicking square dance.

In the interval everyone went out on the lawn to enjoy the barbecue of sausages and steak sandwiches, luscious and smoky with long cool glasses of hock or lemonade. Joanna was the centre of a group who wanted to hear all about the 'old country'. Several of the valley wives had parents who had come to Australia as emigrants, and she was plied with eager questions about places she had never actually seen.

'I'm a country girl,' she laughed. 'No, I haven't lunched on the roof of the G.P.O. Tower . . . no, it really isn't cold all the time. We've had some lovely summers . . . yes, women are allowed to have a drink in our pubs. . . . Englishmen don't mind at all!'

It was a relief when a stockman began to play a tune on his guitar and to sing a song that told of a bushranger who fell in love and was a good man till the day his 'little gal' went searching the bush for a wandering piccaninny and was seen no more. The bushranger looked high and low for her, but she was seen no more.

'You all alone, Miss Joanna?'

Joana glanced round and met the lopsided grin of Tye Jennings. 'Vance wanted a few words with his aunt.' She smiled. 'Are all stock-riding songs so sad?'

'Riding round the cattle at night can be a mite lonely and that gets into the songs. These are mighty good sausages!'

'Mmmm.' Her eyes shone bright by the glow of the nearby coals under the grill of the barbecue, the dancing and the sense of excitement had sharpened her appetite. 'I could eat enother hot dog. How about you, Tye?'

He nodded and they went over to help themselves from the platter of smoking sausages and the basket of rolls. Bushy was assisting with the barbecue, having been a first-rate camp cook in his time. He looked piratical with the glow of the coals on his seamed face.

'Where have you put the mustard?' Tye wanted to know.

'Do you need any, young feller, with a pretty girl in tow?' Bushy chuckled at his own joke and winked at Joanna. 'It's over on that table with the bread and pickles.'

Tye was laughing as he stepped over a log seat and reached for the jar of mustard. Joanna went to say something to Bushy, and it was then there was a sizzle, a sudden spurt of flame in the fat-pan and the next instant some grease on Bushy's big apron caught the flame and jabbed her to shock and action in the same instant. The apron was the sort that tied at the back and even as Bushy's face contorted with fear, Joanna was behind him and fumbling with the strings. Then she gave a gasp, echoed by a curse, as something doused both her and Bushy in a chilly foam, and she saw a tall figure standing over them with a gleaming extinguisher in his hands.

'Oh – heavens!' She brushed at the foam, while Bushy

gave a hoarse, still frightened chuckle.

'First time I ever had a lady risk her neck for my leathery hide. Missy, you all right?'

'Yes, I think so – it brushes off.'

'The pair of you could have been as barbecued as those beefsteaks.' The deep voice lashed at them. 'What were you playing at, Bushy?'

'Weren't my fault, Boss. The fat got in the fire and caught my apron. Missy here was helping old one-arm.'

'Joanna . . .?'

She looked up all the way to the stern face of Adam Corraine, still a bit shivery, and deeply startled to hear her name on his lips. Not gently by any means, but as if he were a trifle concerned.

'You were quick, Boss.' Bushy was fingering the burn hole in his apron, while people clustered round and flung questions, and looked askance at the fire extinguisher Adam was holding.

'Good thing we keep one of these on the veranda.' He gestured at the barn-hall with its wooden posts and lattice-work. 'I was coming out for some food and I heard Miss Dowling cry out.'

'Did I?' Joanna looked at him with large eyes and wondered what it was she had cried out. A name perhaps . . . *his* name? Anyway, it had been effective and he had come swiftly to their rescue. 'It's a good thing your reactions are such swift ones, Mr. Corraine.'

'Yes,' he said laconically. He turned to the crowd. 'Let's get back to the music and the dancing, everyone. The mishap is over, and there's still an hour of fun left in the evening.'

Friendly hands patted Joanna on the shoulder, and then someone almost as tall as Adam came thrusting through the crowd to her side. 'Joanna, what happened?'

'Miss Dowling and Bushy decided to liven up the party.' There was a sardonic smile on the Boss's lips as he strolled away, still carrying the extinguisher.

'You want some tucker, Boss,' Bushy called out.

'A steak sandwich, Bushy.'

'I'll bring it, Boss. Any pickles?'

A sardonic laugh came floating back to them, while Vance questioned in a low voice and the music started up again in the hall.

'Yes, he'll have some pickles with it,' Bushy muttered, and all at once Joanna felt like laughing and crying. There was nothing tame, nothing easily known about Adam Corraine. He withheld his secret self, and loped up the steps of the veranda with the silence and suppleness of a man who never panicked. Boss of Raintree. What would the place be without him?

'My dress,' she said, for though the foam had brushed off it had left marks on the pale material. 'If you don't mind, Vance, I'd like to go back to the house.'

'Sure, honey, I'll take you.'

'I'd like to walk.' Suddenly she wanted to be alone and quiet. 'You stay and enjoy the dance.'

'Not without you, Joanna.'

'Vance!'

It was Bonney, running across the lawn with the light of the lanterns turning her to a fairy thing. 'Vance and Joanna, you're to come in and dance. And Bushy, the Boss wants his steak sandwich.'

'I'm coming with it, right now.' Bushy ambled off, carrying the sandwich and two dill pickles on a plate. A life of sudden alarms and nerves built to take them had not left him as shaken as Joanna. She shrank from going back into that brightly lit hall, where all eyes would be upon her ... heroine of the hour who wanted to hide away.

'Go and dance with Bonney,' she urged. 'I feel like a quiet walk, Vance. The night air will cool my head.'

'Joanna ...'

'Please.' The sound of strain was in her voice. 'I'm all on edge, prickly, like a cat that's had a scare. Don't insist on coming with me.'

'You know the way?' He looked uncertain, his hair rumpled from the dancing, hunched over her a little, as if to pluck her wilful slenderness close to him. 'You weren't hurt in any way, Joanna?'

She shook her head. 'It was all too quick for that – like a dream. Bonney, dance with him!'

She turned away without further argument and hastened from the poppy-like girl and the man whose shoulder it would have been good to lean against, some other time. She made for the road that led past the bungalows to the hill crowned by the homestead. A tethered horse rattled his harness, and the music hung on the air with the smell of trees and the nutty tang of the many head of cattle, guarded down there on the range by the stockmen on duty. Boye Dawson among them. Lenita had not been at the dance ... a young wife and mother, too much in love to dance with anyone but Boye.

Joanna saw the light on in the Dawson bungalow, but she passed by, smiling a little as she saw the moonlight agleam on the steel supports of baby Carlo's swing. Little house of love, with blue shutters.

She left the lights behind, and the drifting music, and all was still but for herself moving along through the night with the young moon, a curve of pale gold against the velvet dark sky. The outlines of the homestead came into view and she paused beside the white gate and listened as a dog barked.

Was it a dog or a dingo, prowling around in the hope of stealing a chicken? She leaned against the five-barred gate, too spent to go further and at peace after the turmoil down on the lawn of the barn-hall. Oh dear, what had she got herself into? Viviana was miles away, and she was a lone English girl at Raintree, at the mercy of a gentle heart, and unprepared by her twenty-odd years with Gran for men as charming as Vance . . . men as iron-strong and masterful as Adam Corraine.

She took a deep breath of the night air, and on impulse she loosed her hair from its chignon and let the wind blow it back from her temples. So good, the free wild scents from the valley. She climbed the gate and sat on the top bar, ash-blonde and still in the moonlight. A breeze came whispering in her ears: *'Call her once and come away.'*

She smiled at the fancy, and then something made her turn her head and her heart quickened as a tall figure came quietly towards her. 'Vance?' Even as she spoke the name, she knew with all her nerves that only one man moved with such deliberation, as if the very soles of his feet had love for the soil of Raintree. The pale light of the moon shone on the lean strength of his face and showed the glint of mastery in his eyes.

'Was it you who called me?' She heard her own voice with surprise and the words it spoke.

'The line came to me – it seemed appropriate.' He drew near and his tallness brought his eyes level with hers, where she sat on the gate. 'You didn't come back to the dance – Aunt Charly was a little worried about you, and dancing is something I can take or leave alone.'

'Are you asking me if I'm all right, Mr. Corraine?' A smile just touched her lips, a nervous little appeal that he

84

smile in return, just once.

His glance played over her as he propped a foot upon the rails of the gate and leaned his forearm against his thigh. 'You might have got burned and run off like a young cat to lick your wound in secret.'

'Do you think I'm a secretive person, Mr. Corraine?'

'You're a deep one, Miss Dowling.'

She gazed back at him, caught between the keen silver of his eyes and the night all around. They had never been so alone and she tried to hide behind her lashes from the strength that made her feel as helpless as that branch of mimosa Aunt Charly had talked about.

'You acted too quickly for any real damage to be done – except to my dress. These light materials show marks easily, that was why I wouldn't dance any more. Sheer female vanity.'

'Is the dress a total write-off?'

'As my best one, which it was. But after a good wash it will do for everyday.'

'I caused the damage, so I'll replace it.'

'No, there's really no need. I'm only too glad that Bushy wasn't hurt. He tries so hard to be useful with that one arm—'

'He was a good all-round man in his day. A bit of a wanderer when younger, but whenever he turned up at Raintree for work my grandfather always took him on.'

'He's deeply grateful that you let him stay on at Raintree. I think to live here is to love the valley.'

'I thought women were more concerned with loving a man?'

'There are several loves in a woman's life, as there are in a man's.'

'Have you known other men beside my cousin?'

She stared at Adam, and suddenly the wind felt cold.

His question had been deliberate, not casual, and he had followed her not from concern but to harp back to the early part of the evening, when he had come upon her just as Vance had taken forcible hold of her.

'There was the boy who cleaned out the pig run for us, and old Jack who pruned the trees in the orchard. Then there was the butcher and the baker—'

She broke off with a cry as in that quick way of his Adam took her wrist in a grip impossible to break. 'Don't be clever with me,' he said, and she felt the muted thunder in him, the whisper of lightning. 'Vance isn't for you, and you aren't for him!'

'I never said—'

'You said he proposed to you.'

'He meant it as a joke—'

'A funny thing to joke about. Don't you regard marriage as a serious matter, Miss Dowling?'

'Of course I do—'

'Then you can take my word for it that you won't marry my cousin if I can prevent it.'

'Your arrogance is beyond belief,' she gasped. 'You can't boss people around as if they're cattle.'

'I can make sure they don't wander in the wrong direction.'

'Meaning?'

'That Vance is wandering and I don't like it.'

It took her breath away that he should say it outright ... his cool nerve was something to marvel at a moment before she lost her temper. 'Anyone can see that you're hidebound by family pride and property, and so you think every female stranger is out to become a part of your illustrious family. All I want is a job, for as long as it takes me to earn enough to pay my fare to New Zealand. That's what I came for, funnily enough, Mr. Corraine, not

86

to find a wealthy Australian husband!'

When she said that, his fingers tightened for a painful moment on her wrist and she became conscious of how close he was, so that she felt the warmth of his physique ... warmer than his heart, with its plans all made for those who belonged to Raintree.

'I've made my plans as well, Mr. Corraine. I'm saving my wages so I can join my sister as soon as possible.'

'Have you heard from her?'

'Not yet, but I wrote to her before I left Sydney and she knows I'm here. I took the liberty of assuming that I'd be suitable as a home-help.'

'Miss Dowling—'

'I felt your dislike of me from the moment we met, Mr. Corraine. First you took me for a gold-digger, now you're worried in case your cousin marries the kitchen help. You also must take me for a little idiot if you think I don't know when a man is playing at love.' She gave a laugh that was half angry, half genuinely amused. 'You really seem very mixed up about me. I'm just an ordinary girl with no wish in the world to disrupt your household or your plans for Vance.'

'Not all that ordinary,' he drawled. 'Bushy would strike some girls as just an old one-armed codger who lives in the past.'

'He's rather lonely and divided from his family – I just happen to understand how he feels.' Feeling the slack of Adam's fingers she broke free of his touch, jumped down off the gate and ran away from him towards the house. It hurt to be misjudged, and despite her growing attachment to Raintree she wished she had enough money so she could fly away to Viviana. Suddenly she felt all choked up. It was true what she had said about the loneliness of being divided from loved ones. It overwhelmed her, coming on the heels of her fight with Adam Corraine, and tears filled her eyes and she blundered into a ghost-gum before she saw it.

'Oh—' It seemed like the last straw, and as Adam loomed she cried out: 'Don't touch me – I couldn't bear it!'

'Are you hurt?' His voice sounded very distant and curt.

'No.' She ran on, into the house, and when she reached her room she flung herself across the bed and cried for home. Why had she left everything that was familiar to her, and loved? Why hadn't she taken Gran's advice and gone to work at the livery stable for Ian MacLean? 'That lad likes you,' Gran had said. 'He makes a fair living out of the riding school, and a young woman can't ask for more than kindness and a bit of jam on her bread.'

Couldn't she? Joanna wondered as she propped herself on her elbow and wiped the tears from her cheeks. A bit of security and a taste of jam seemed rather poor things in comparison to a dream of love so warm and vital and un-assailable that nothing outside that strong rim of love could ever really hurt a girl.

Unusual thoughts for her to be having, and she found herself listening for the sound of footfalls in the house. All was quiet, and on impulse she went to the window and opened it carefully a little wider. There drifted upwards on the night air the aroma of tobacco smoke, and she knew the Boss was down there on the rear veranda, smoking his pipe and gazing at the mountains that guarded the valley.

It was an overwhelming thought that all the territory for miles around was Adam Corraine's, handed on to him by his grandfather, to be handed on in his turn to . . . ?

Joanna's heart beat faster than it should.

'My cousin is a born bachelor,' Vance had said. 'He must take a bride ... or see Raintree go to a son of mine.'

Was that the answer to Adam's arrogant behaviour down by the paddock gate? Did he plan to stay solitary and was taking it upon himself to select the mother for Vance's son? It seemed very feudal, and yet the idea fitted in with the atmosphere at Raintree. The place was cut off from civilization, and Adam had been reared almost exclusively by a hard, proud, exacting man whom everyone had called King. It wasn't so far-fetched really, that Adam should have made plans into which the girl stranger from England didn't fit.

She took a troubled heart to bed with her ... she hadn't dreamed that Adam Corraine thought so little of her that he couldn't tolerate the idea of Vance loving her.

Whatever Adam Corraine's private feelings, he kept his promise about the pony and Brindle was available for horseback riding whenever Joanna was free of her household duties for an hour or so.

She loved Brindle from the moment she mounted him and he did a little dance to let her know that he had some pepper in him. The saddle was a slightly worn one of Bonney's, so it fitted her, but the stirrup leathers hung rather long and it was Adam who came to her side to shorten them. He glanced up at her and his look was a long, unsmiling one. 'Now you should ride more comfortably.'

'Thank you.' She smiled diffidently. 'I *can* ride ... there's no need to look at me as if I'm about to topple out of the saddle.'

Bonney's pony Satin suddenly pranced, as if the girl tightened her grip on the bridle. Like Joanna she wore

89

narrow trousers and a cotton shirt, with a slouch hat as protection against the sun. But around her neck there floated a scarlet chiffon scarf. She seemed fond of the colour as if it expressed a hint of fire in her temperament.

'Have I got to look out for Joanna?' she drawled. 'I thought it was the companion's job to look after me.'

Joanna tilted her chin, and the slouch of her hat made her eyes sparkle deep blue with challenge. 'It does sound Edwardian to be called a companion, as if I should be wearing a full skirt and sitting side-saddle.'

She gave a laugh and felt the flick of masculine eyes over her slacks and shirt, a smoky blue colour with neat collar and cuffs. 'Off with the pair of you. And if you ride in the forest, Bonney, don't go too far.'

'You'd have to come looking for us, Boss, if we went astray.' Bonney gave him a saucy look from her saddle. 'You'd be so annoyed at being taken away from your precious work, wouldn't you? Or would you send Vance to search for us?'

'Would you prefer Vance to rescue you?' He took Bonney's bridle and led her pony out of the stable. Joanna followed on Brindle, and the sun was warm, ripening the smell of horses and hay. She heard Bonney laugh softly.

'As if I'd prefer anyone but you, Adam – you are the first man!'

Joanna felt his gaze upon them as they cantered away from the homestead, and she knew there was a smile deep in the sky-grey eyes, a gleam of sunshine and warmth aroused by his pretty and impudent ward – who seemed to be a little in love with him.

The sun flared across Corraine's land like living gold, and a little way off Joanna saw a mob of kangaroos feeding among the woollybutts. Adam allowed small mobs of

90

them on his property, and they certainly added a touch of charm and strangeness, like big rabbits up on their hind legs and hopping about with a sort of lovable clumsiness.

Bonney turned in her saddle and gave Joanna an inquiring look. 'Do you want to see the forest?' she asked.

'I wouldn't mind seeing a part of it, but we'd better not go too far.'

'Are you afraid of the Boss?'

'No. But if it's possible to get lost in the rain-forest, then I'd sooner not tempt fate.'

'It's fun to tempt.' Bonney gave a laugh. 'That's what women are for, otherwise it's all cooking and drudgery. I'd hate to work at what you do.'

'You'll do a certain amount of it when you're married,' Joanna pointed out.

'Not me! The help can run the home. I'm not going to wear myself out and not be attractive any more to – to the man I marry.'

'I take it he'll have money?' Joanna found herself amused by the girl, who spoke a lot like Viviana, and who had the same assurance about her prettiness and what it could do for her.

'I wouldn't want to be poor. I'd hate that more than anything.'

'What if the man you loved lost all his money?'

'I wouldn't marry him. Being awfully poor makes a woman plain, and I'd hate that as well. When you're pretty people like you, and let you have the things you want. Is it so bad to want nice things, and people being kind and pleasant to you?'

'It's perfectly natural, Bonney, but a kindness of heart has to go with a pretty face or it loses the glow that makes a flower bloom in the sun.'

'Our kind of sun can kill a flower,' Bonney taunted. 'They bloom much more richly in the shadow of the forest. Orchids as big as a man's hand, and gorgeous flame flowers – but I suppose your favourite is the rose – as you're English.'

'Yes, I have a love of roses.' Joanna smiled. 'We had a bush of them in the front garden of our cottage back home. Apricot-coloured tea-roses that grew in such clusters that their scent seemed to burst in through the windows and drench the house from morning till night.'

'You sound homesick.' Bonny looked curious. 'Why did you come to Raintree? Was it to be with Vance?'

'No! Good heavens, I needed a job. When Vance met me at Hawk's Bay I was down to my last couple of pounds.'

'You danced a lot with Vance at last Saturday's frolic.'

'We're good friends,' Joanna said quickly. 'It doesn't mean because two people dance together that they're madly in love. Sometimes people in love are too shy to even look at each other in company.'

Bonney stared at Joanna, and suddenly her young mouth was sulky. 'You talk like a schoolmarm, and look like one with your hair pulled back in a nape knot. Don't kid me you didn't come to Queensland looking for a husband. Everyone in the valley reckons so.'

'Then everyone in the valley is wrong. I'm saving up to go to New Zealand, and now shall we have a short canter in the forest before I have to get back to my chores?'

'You really mean to join your sister?'

'I can't wait.' Joanna met the girl's eyes and saw them sparkling. So one more member of the Corraine clan would be glad to see her go! She gripped the rein and Brindle broke into a gallop. Before she knew what was happening he was heading for the hills that swept down to the cattle run, and because she was still a stranger to him he wouldn't obey when she tugged on the reins. He had got his head and a sniff of the pasturage, and his hoofs pounded the ground as he carried her downhill at such a pace that her slouch hat blew off her head and she could see the rusty shapes of cattle looming ever nearer.

'Brindle . . . whoa!'

The pony took not a bit of heed, and suddenly the pair of them were on the range of the cattle and one of the stockmen was riding full tilt at a bull and it was swerving towards Joanna. A great lumbering creature with fire in its eye, coming straight for Joanna and the pony, and the next moment halted in its tracks as the stockman leapt from his horse and grabbed the bull by the tail.

Joanna saw this as Brindle galloped on, and then she felt the pony stumble and the next moment she was flying out of the saddle, the breath knocked out of her as she landed in a spinifex bush.

'Ouch!' She scrambled to her feet and felt stung, bumped and breathless. She rubbed her behind and then looked up slowly as a shadow loomed over her. She half expected to see the scrub bull, and it was almost as disconcerting to find the Boss looking at her.

CHAPTER FIVE

'ENJOY your ride?' He sat his horse against the sun and looked down at her from the saddle of the chestnut.

'Exhilarating.' She felt herself blushing and bent her head as she brushed at her trousers. Brindle stood a little way off, cropping the grass and flicking his tail with careless indifference. She bit her lip ... it was extra maddening that Adam should be out stockriding and a witness to her tumble.

'How come you're down this far getting tossed into a spinifex bush?' he asked laconically. 'And where's Bonney?'

Of course, he would be more concerned for that young lady! Joanna looked him in the eye and forgot the flush in her cheeks. 'Bonney was taking me to see the rain-forest when the pony broke loose and brought me down here on the range. Like everyone else at Raintree he takes me for a lemon, but I'll learn, Mr. Corraine.'

His eyes flicked her soft tousled hair. It had come loose from its chignon and the sun was stroking its fairness. Her fall had half pulled the shirt out of the waistband of her slacks, and there was a smudge of dirt across her forehead where she had pushed her hair out of her eyes.

The smile at the edge of his mouth told her what an urchin she looked. 'You're green all right,' he drawled, 'but gritty with it.'

Even as she felt a stab of confused pleasure at what, for him, was a compliment, a stockman rode up and Joanna recognized him as the one who had thrown the bull. He stared at Joanna, then spoke to the Boss. 'I cut that clear-

94

skin out of the herd, Boss. Missy here nearly got in his way.' It was a laconic understatement that carried all the weight of what might have happened to her if he had been less prompt in dealing with the bull. His hat was pushed to the back of his forehead and his face was shiny from the heat of his exertions. He was a young man, and had rather nice eyes set round with the sunray of lines that somehow increased the attraction of these men who lived most of their lives in the open.

'Thank you for what you did,' Joanna said gratefully.

'My pleasure, miss.' He grinned shyly. 'You got to be firm with man and beast in this part of the world, and I guess that pony fooled you into thinking him docile because he's so neat and pretty.'

'He must have helped to win many a *chukka*,' she smiled, aware of Adam up there on the raking chestnut he handled so firmly with his lean, sun-bitten hands.

'You know about polo?' The young stockman looked impressed.

'I saw a game played at Windsor Park once.'

'You mean Prince Philip was playing?'

'Yes, it was marvellous.'

'Can you beat that?' The stockman's eyes were bright against his sun-tanned face. 'Wait till I tell Nita—'

'Right now, Boye,' Adam drawled, 'we'll join the others for smoko. I expect you could go a cup of tea, Miss Dowling, after your little adventure?'

'Yes,' her response was heartfelt, for a cup of tea seemed always to lighten a burden and it felt like one, to be always in scrapes like a schoolgirl instead of a reliable home-help.

Adam swung from his saddle and hooked the reins over a nearby branch so Blaze could crop the grass in company with her pony, who looked so innocent, the devil, with his silky mane and tail, and his head cocked in her direction as if very pleased with himself for getting his own way. Jackeroo! He tossed his mane and nuzzled the wheat-warm grass again.

Joanna walked with Adam and Boye, to where a fire had been made to boil the large billy-can, into which a couple of handfuls of tea would be tossed, to brew smoky and brown over the flames. Boye squatted, a leg stretched out as he rolled a cigarette. Adam leaned against a tree, a hand in the narrow belt of his trousers, his boots crossed at the ankles and mellowed to a goldy shade. He seemed to blend in with his background, strong and alert, the lightning play of his glance on his men, his cattle, his sun-golden lands that stretched to the mountains.

The air was so good, primitive somehow with its nutty tang of animals and woodsmoke. Joanna breathed it in, and her bruises and scratches, her hair in fair disorder, made her feel sixteen again. It was just after her sixteenth birthday that she discarded youthful pranks for the cares of an early womanhood. Viviana had run away from the farm and left her to be Gran's solace and companion, at work, and in the evenings when other girls were invited out to the cinema or a local dance. She hadn't minded too much. A girl doesn't question duty when it's done out of affection, and Joanna had always been fond of her grand-mother, even in her stern moods.

Life with Gran on the smallholding, and the scent of summer roses, seemed part of another time. This was the reality, a mug of campfire tea enjoyed in the company of sun-weathered men with rugged faces and eyes with a faraway look in them.

Joanna drank deep of her tea ... bravado alone had made her tell Bonney that she couldn't wait to get away from Raintree. She knew in her heart that love of the place had already taken root there, and it would be a wrench when the time came to uproot herself. Right now she dug her heels into Corraine soil, felt on her lips the tang of open places, and the sudden impact of sky-grey eyes as she tilted her head. That gaze was disturbing. It stirred the memory of the night he had said grimly that she wasn't for Vance.

Was Adam remembering that night as he lounged at his ease against a tree? There seemed to be a glint way back in his eyes, but as always it was impossible to tell what he was thinking. It was a strange fact that his eyes were made inscrutable by their clearness, as a pool is when sunlight flashes across its surface. Was he laughing at her a little, for thinking she could become a permanent part of Raintree? Or was it mere male amusement at the way she had been tossed into a spinifex bush?

She finished her tea and handed back the mug. 'I'd better be getting back to the homestead,' she said. 'You boys don't want to have to wait for your tucker.'

Boye Dawson gave her a grin. 'You're getting to talk like one of us, Miss Joanna.'

'Thank you for saying so.' She smiled at Boye and felt the Boss looking at her. 'But I think it will be some time before I stop being the jackeroo around here.'

'We could do with a few more cut from the same pattern,' drawled Tye, the young stockman who had pearled the waters off the coral islands, and who fetched her pony across to her, docile now with a belly full of grass. Tye gave her a hand into the saddle, but Adam Corraine was no longer there to take heed with eyes that saw everything and gave nothing away. He had strolled off to talk to his foreman, and Joanna cantered off in the other direction, escorted by Tye until they were clear of the cattle.

'Can I come up to the house this evening and talk with you on the back veranda?' he asked.

She was about to give him a lighthearted yes, when she remembered that she mustn't become involved with any of Corraine's men. He wanted none of that sort of trouble, and though Tye was a nice boy, mere friendship with him was ruled out by the very way they were placed up here at Raintree. Miles from a town, from the gay and attactive girls who could be flirted with for a few hours without other people getting the idea that a romance was in the air.

According to Bonney the valley community believed that Joanna was out to land a husband, and she didn't wish to add fuel to the wagging tongues.

'After that toss into a bush I've got a date with a shampoo,' she said lightly. 'Sorry, Tye.'

'In other words,' he said wryly, 'I'd be treading on someone's corns.'

'I don't quite—'

'It's Vance Corraine, isn't it? He'd be the big catch around here – next to the Boss, and everyone knows that he's a loner and has his heartstrings tied to Raintree.'

Her heart gave a queer lurch as she looked at Tye, his slouch hat pushed back off his forehead and his good-looking face storm-clouded. 'I wish you people wouldn't assume so much,' she broke out. 'Let me do my own thinking and feeling. I'm not out to catch *anyone*, do you understand? And if you're lonely for company, Tye, why not ask Bonney to walk and talk with you?'

'She's a bit too stuck up for me,' he retorted. 'That little madam wouldn't give the time of day to a feller.'

'She's very pretty, Tye.'

'Sure, like the tree-fern that hides a stinging-bush!'

'Don't exaggerate.' Joanna gave a laugh. 'She may be shy with young men. Some girls are, and they develop a kind of father fixation about older men.'

'You mean the Boss?'

'Y-yes, I suppose I do.'

'Bonney Ryan doesn't look upon the Boss as a father!' Tye swung his horse around and prepared to gallop away. 'She'd like to marry him and become missus of Raintree ... and maybe she'll get her wish, though he's a loner, like everyone says. A man with all this land, and one of the finest herds this side of Queensland, has got to think about the future, and King Corraine before him married a pretty young thing just to make sure the heritage went to a Corraine. Me? All I've got to offer a girl is a friendly nature and a warm heart. I reckon the Boss has a heart like those eyes of his – distant as the skies to touch!'

Tye rode off, and Joanna sat her pony on a hill that overlooked the range where the sleek roan cattle roamed and fed. The sun shone down upon her, but she felt curiously cold. A heart as distant as the skies to touch. Bonney was not to be envied, if her wish was to win the Boss of Raintree. But maybe Bonney was the type of girl to be satisfied with position and possessions. Maybe a strong and passionate love was not her hunger.

Joanna touched her heels to Brindle and he cantered on towards the house, that basked in all its pleasant, mellow-walled proportions among the shade trees. She hadn't known until coming here, until perhaps a few minutes ago, that it was her own hunger, to share with a man a love so strong and warm that the world itself could never offer more delight.

The coldness went and her cheeks felt warm in the stables as she made Brindle comfortable, and then went indoors to wash and change before helping to prepare the chops, onions and roast potatoes for dinner – not forgetting the fruit pies with lashings of custard.

It was good to get to work. To lose herself in the spicy atmosphere of the big kitchen, where the two girls talked softly together over the mound of potatoes they were peeling, and the drone of bees drifted in with the scent of gum-tree blossoms.

All at once the peace was shattered as the door breezed open and a tall figure filled the kitchen with wide shoulders and the ring of spurs. 'I need some first aid!' It was Vance, his right hand bound in his neckcloth, which was rusty with blood.

'Bring the box, Peg!'

Joanna steered the patient to the sink, where he let his makeshift bandage be unwound by her deft fingers. She caught her breath at the jagged cut in the palm of his hand. 'It's deep, Vance!' She held his hand under the cold water, but the bleeding wouldn't stop and she looked up anxiously into his blue eyes. 'How did you do it?'

'Barbed wire. Give me a pack of cottonwool and I'll grip on it.'

'Right.' She took the first-aid box from Peg, who watched with big eyes as Joanna pulled open a packet of cottonwool and tore off a chunk for Vance to grip against the tear in his hand. She saw him wince and suggested that one of the girls make a pot of coffee. In no time at all he was settled in a chair with the girls buzzing around him, waiting on his every whim.

'It looks worse than it is,' he said calmly. 'I'm a full-blooded lad, remember.'

He winked at Joanna, who refused to treat the matter as a joke. 'You wouldn't care to be like Bushy, now would you? Now please keep still and let me fix this bandage—'

'Two arms are better than one,' he murmured, his un-injured arm stealing around her waist.

'Vance, behave!' She tended to him with the same concern she would have shown anyone in trouble, but as she bent over him she looked very fair against his tanned ruggedness, and he wouldn't remove his arm from around her. She saw a shadow and knew they were observed, and a quiver ran through her fingers as she secured the bandage.

The Boss stood just inside the screen door, a sardonic look on his face as he surveyed the chaos in routine created by his handsome cousin. Not a potato had been set to roast, and the onions bobbed about in the bowl waiting for the slicer. Instead of domestic order there was a strew of antiseptic, cottonwool and coffee cups.

'So what happened?' drawled Adam. 'Did you leave a finger on the wire, or was it a whole hand?'

Joanna looked up quickly. 'There's no need to be funny,' she said, stung on Vance's behalf. 'We've had a job to stop the cut from bleeding.'

'That bad?' Adam quizzed his cousin, taking in his ruffled hair, slight smile, and bandaged hand.

'A cow had her hoof through the wire and I got torn getting her free.'

Adam frowned. 'Your right hand, I notice.'

'It might be okay with a glove on.' Vance's smile was valiant.

'No, rest the hand for a day or so.' Adam turned to leave the kitchen. 'I'll put Boye in charge of branding the young stock – and Miss Dowling, if your patient is well enough to walk will you shoo him out of your way and get dinner organized?'

'Right away, sir.'

He gave her a long look over his shoulder, and then he

sauntered away – but she could have sworn there had been a gleam of amusement in his grey eyes.

In the next couple of days Vance made the most of his injury. Joanna had to dress it for him – he said her cool and soothing touch was working wonders – and afterwards he stretched out in a long chair on the veranda and yarned with Aunt Charly, or argued with Bonney.

Joanna heard them as she sat in the cool of the dining-room polishing the family silver, evocative to handle because it had been wrought from the treasure found in a ship sunk off the Great Barrier Reef. She liked the gleam of it in her fingers, and the thrilling fact that long ago it had lain in the coffers of some Spanish or Dutch pirate. It seemed typical that a Corraine should take it for his own to adorn the table at Raintree ... on special occasions.

Bonney had a birthday at the week-end and there was to be a party for her. Aunt Charly had suggested to Adam that they use the silver, and he had agreed with an indulgent smile to do the thing in style. Joanna had been given the task of cleaning it, but because of its beauty and its history she didn't find the work tedious. Adoniah, the headmaster of the valley school, had promised roses for the silver bowl, and an iced cake and other goodies were coming by aeroplane on Friday – and no doubt a very special gift from Adam would be among the packages.

He had said firmly that Bonney was not yet ready to have a car of her own. Raintree was so many miles off the main highway that she could lose herself, or have a break-down and be stranded. No, he was responsible for her until she came of age, and with that sudden switch from demand to demureness the girl had touched a hand to his sun-lined cheek and given in to him.

'Bossy Adam,' she had said, her brown eyes fixed on his

face, and every eye in the lounge fixed on the couple last night as if fascinated. 'What a demanding husband you're going to make!'

His answer to that provocative remark had been to clamp his pipe in his mouth and puff a screen of smoke, but the sudden bright pink in Bonney's cheeks had seemed to indicate that they had a secret he was not yet ready to share with the family. With a faintly nervous laugh the girl had put a record on the radiogram and hummed the tune while the others talked of this and that. But there had been tension in the room, a current of awareness rippling from person to person, and Joanna could almost smell again the tang of tobacco smoke mingling with the night flowers that gave off their scent in the darkness beyond the homestead.

The scents were less apparent in sunlight, and as she glossed the silver with a soft rag she could hear Vance talking to Bonney in a lazy, teasing voice. 'I suppose you're hoping for lots of loot on Saturday, eh? What would you like me to give you?'

'Do you mean you haven't ordered me a present from town?' the girl exclaimed. 'In that case I'll go without. I don't want some old thing you forgot to give to one of your girl-friends.'

'Hold on, I haven't a string of the fillies,' he laughed. 'They're passing acquaintances who add a bit of light and laughter.'

'Does the same go for Joanna Dowling?'

Joanna paused in her work as she caught her name on Bonney's lips, and she found herself sitting tensed for Vance's reply. Would he jest, or reveal something she would rather not hear? Don't, she wanted to cry out. Nothing can come of what I feel, or what you feel. We left our chance behind at Hawk's Bay.

'I think you're jealous of Joanna,' he drawled.

'You're soft about her because she has blonde hair and a lah-di-dah voice. I think she's stuck-up!'

'Don't be a child,' he laughed lazily. 'Joanna is a nice girl. She isn't a greedy, selfish little dolly like you – ouch, you throw another nectarine at me and I'll tan your—' Suddenly there came the sound of a chair being thrust back, a scramble, a yelp, and then the laughter faded as Vance chased Bonney across the lawn and in among the trees. A parakeet let out a squawk, and silence prevailed as Joanna slowly relaxed in her chair at the table spread with Corraine silver.

It was a relief to be invited to spend the evening with Lenita and her husband. Their bungalow was as delightful inside as out, with gay furnishings to which things from Italy added a warm charm, like the colour of Lenita's hair and skin against Boye's fairness. To see the couple together was to feel their love for each other, and Joanna fell a willing victim to the plump good looks of young Carlo. To hold him was a pleasure and a novelty, for after bathing him Lenita allowed Joanna to dry and powder him, and tuck him up for the night.

As she leaned over the cot the night light gleamed on her hair and Carlo reached for the shining strand and she gave a laughing gasp of pain and pleasure.

'You no longer gather your hair at the nape,' said Lenita as she loosed her son's strong young grip on Joanna's hair.

'No.' Joanna smiled down into Carlo's huge dark eyes. 'It might be safer to go back to it . . . the old urge to grab a girl by the hair seems to linger in the male of the species. Carlo *mio*, you're going to be quite a lad when you grow up.'

Carlo gurgled an affirmative, and his skin was soft and

warm as Joanna bent and kissed him. '*Buona sera, bello bambino,*' she murmured.

They left the nursery and joined Boye in the lounge, where he was waiting to pour them a drink. 'What do you think of the son of the house?' he smiled.

'He's gorgeous.' Joanna sank back against a cushion with her drink. She wore a casual grey-blue dress with a square lace collar that revealed the pale delicacy of her throat. Her pale gold hair was a soft curve on her shoulders, with a central parting that gave her a look of demureness.

'It's nice for Nita to have you for a friend,' Boye said sincerely. He gestured at the kitchen, from whence came the clatter of dishes and the appetizing aroma of an Italian sauce. 'She's the best, but I worry about her when I have to be away for the mustering. Now and then she gets homesick for Italy just as you must get a longing for your home and family in England. Most of the other women on the station are Australians. They're born to living beyond the blue, but it's hard for Nita when she gets a longing for the colour and bustle of a Roman market place, and the streets with houses set so close a couple of girls can gossip across the street without moving from their windowsills.'

Boye studied the drink in his hand and looked sombre for a moment. 'I've thought of taking Nita back to Italy and settling down there, but this job here at Raintree Valley is the best I've ever had. There isn't a boss for thousands of miles as good as Adam Corraine. He pays fair and he acts fair, and in a few years if I want to branch out on my own he'll help me. This is a land of opportunity. Maybe not beautiful like Italy . . .'

'I understand what you mean, Boye.'

'You do?' His eyes were eager on Joanna's face. 'You

think I'm right to keep this job – you think Nita understands?'

'She loves you,' Joanna said simply. 'I don't suppose she pines for her homeland as much as you think she does. You and Carlo are her world – anyone can see that.'

'She's mine,' Boye said frankly. 'I'd give up living and working here if I thought Nita really wanted that . . .'

'But I don't!' Lenita had entered the room so swiftly that she caught Boye in mid-sentence. 'Signor husband, will you please not to worry because once in a while I get a little ache for the old country. Joanna knows! It lasts but a little time and then it is gone. My life is here with you . . . a few memories are not important.'

'Nita—'

'I will fetch the dinner.' With a smile she was gone, to reappear almost at once with a large dish of spaghetti lavishly sprinkled with sauce and cheese. With laughing eyes Lenita assured her husband that she was not being nostalgic; she merely wished to show off her skill as an Italian cook. Apart from which Joanna must be browned off with steak and eggs!

'How did you guess?' The aroma of the spaghetti sauce teased Joanna's nostrils, and she enjoyed every mouthful of the Italian food and the red wine.

Afterwards they sat out on the small veranda, where it was good to breathe the cool air among the cluster of vines growing over the trelliswork. It was a grapevine, and the outline of mangoes could be seen on the trees on the lawn. The Dawsons had a good life and a nice home here in this lovely valley . . . and the voice of a passing dream whispered something that Joanna didn't dare to listen to. Boye strummed his guitar and Lenita talked softly about Carlo. The lights in the other bungalows went out one by one, and still they lingered over their coffee and Boye amused Joanna by telling her about his courtship of Lenita and the fierce protectiveness of her brother. 'Do you know I didn't get to kiss her until *after* the wedding!'

Joanna's laughter rang out. 'Then it isn't true, Boye, that only by a kiss can love be measured?'

'Not in our case, Joanna.' He shot a smile at Lenita. 'One look into those Latin eyes and I was lost anyway. It's the eyes that get a man, and the kissing is all the sweeter from being withheld.'

'Australians are as old-fashioned as Latin men, did you know that, Joanna?' Lenita caressed her husband's face with eyes that sparkled in the half-dark. 'They like a girl to be a home body and it shocks them that women should want more than to run a home.'

'Do you want more, Nita?' There was a smile in Boye's voice.

'I want always what I have now, *caro mio*, but Joanna comes from a land where women run businesses, write books, and go into politics.'

'You a bachelor girl with business plans, Joanna?'

'Hardly.' She gave a laugh, and tried not to feel that flicker of pain about leaving the valley. 'My only plan so far is to join my sister in New Zealand as soon as I can afford the air fare.'

'Is that what you really want?' Lenita murmured.

'It's what I have to do.'

'*Mia* ...'

'All good things have to end some time – like dining here tonight with you and Boye. I've enjoyed every minute ...'

'I'll see you to the homestead, Joanna.'

'That's kind of you, Boye.'

Lenita stood waving good night from the veranda, and

Boye was opening the gate when the roadway gravel crunched beneath a deep tread and someone paused in the half dark and doffed a slouch hat. 'I'm going your way,' said a deep voice, and Joanna looked up at the speaker, a wing of pale hair across her cheek, her eyes wide and startled.

'I don't mind handing over my charge to the Boss,' grinned Boye. 'Good night, Joanna, and thanks for coming to eat with us.'

'Thank you for having me.' Joanna's heart beat rapidly as she waved towards the bungalow, and then fell into step beside Adam Corraine.

'They're a nice couple,' he said.

'Yes, I like them very much.'

'They have a fine youngster.'

'Yes, a real *bello bambino*.'

'You care for children, Miss Dowling?'

'As much as any other single girl, I suppose.'

'It's mainly romance that concerns a young woman, eh?'

'Not every minute of the day.' A smile dented her lips. 'There are times when my sole attention is upon a perfectly baked fruit pie.'

'I have noticed that the fruit pies have improved.'

'I'm planning something special for tomorrow. Aunt Charly has grown a large pumpkin and it seems a shame to let it go to seed.'

'Pumpkins get cooked these days instead of enchanted?'

'Cinderella can always catch a taxi to the ball.'

'Even a monoplane,' he drawled.

Her heart turned slowly over . . . foolish of her to suppose that Adam was being friendly because the night was starry and her fair head reached only to his shoulder. She was the girl who endangered the plans he had made for Vance. He didn't intend to let her forget that a plane had flown her into the valley and could just as easily fly her out.

As he opened the gate to the homestead she stood withdrawn from him, and then as if to tease her a wind blew her hair against Adam's face, an innocent touch she didn't mean to give him. His look flashed down to her, as if her hair had whipped his cheek.

'You usually wear your hair in a roll,' he said.

'A chignon.' She tilted her chin. 'When I'm working, but at the moment I'm off duty and free to wear my hair as I please. I'm sorry it blew in your eyes.'

'It's scented.'

'Shampooed! I – I suppose the kitchen help is entitled to wash the smell of cooking grease out of her tiresome hair?'

'Miss Dowling—'

It sounded treacherously like darling, and all at once the anger and hurt brought tears to her eyes. She blinked rapidly and her lashes felt like small whips. 'Y-you seem to think that I'm full of wiles, Mr. Corraine. Do you think that I'm trying to use them on you?'

'To what purpose?' he drawled.

'Well, you are the master of Raintree. You are the biggest catch.'

'It would take more than golden hair to net me.'

'What would it take?' she asked recklessly. 'I'll risk getting hurt for some things.'

'Who has hurt you?'

'Why, you and the spinifex bush.'

'I haven't touched you – you're just touchy because on the day you arrived at Raintree I thought you wouldn't have the stamina to stand our way of life.'

'Are you saying you're sorry for being wrong about me?'

'Not at all.'

'You mean I haven't yet completed the obstacle course?'

'There's certainly no obstacle in the way of your wit, Miss Dowling. I wonder what it would take to rob you of a retort?' Even as he spoke he caught her by the waist, under the light coat that draped her shoulders, and his hands locked her to his strong, work-supple body, while his eyes mocked the alarm on her star-lit face, pale against her softly blowing hair.

'Lost for a wile?' he mocked.

Her lashes quivered and she was aware with all her senses of the magnetic strength that made it impossible for her to speak or move. At a distance one was aware of the power in this man ... close like this, the hard warmth of his touch right through the soft material of her dress, and she could hardly breathe for the tumult of her heartbeats. *Let me go.* The words clamoured but had no voice. *Please.*

The plea was silent on her lips, but he knew, and with a rough little laugh he let her go. Now only their glances held, and she knew him to be as untamed as the valley and the rain-forest at the heart of it. He wasn't possessive of them because they were his heritage. He was part of them ... they were his Eden.

She backed away from him, and saw the glint of his teeth as he smiled.

'You had to find out just how dangerous I can be. I had to find out just how innocent you are. I think we both learned something, don't you?'

'You know at least that there'll be pumpkin pie for dessert tomorrow.'

He laughed and lounged against the gate-post as Joanna threw him a hurried good night and hastened towards the house. She left him alone with the stars that shone big and gold in the Queensland sky . . . he belonged to the wild wonder of his land as perhaps he could never belong to a woman.

Thursday was a somnolent day, as if everyone drew breath for the bustle to come. Aunt Charly discussed the party menu with Joanna when Bonney was out of ear-shot. 'It's nice for a girl to have an exciting party to re-member.' Charlotte smiled nostalgically. 'I can still recall the thrill of mine when I was eighteen. Ice-cream and strawberries, a dance band, and flattering young men who took you for sugared icing and held you with kid gloves.'

Joanna smiled, even as a pulse quickened in her throat. She seemed to feel again the touch of hands that knew their strength – hands that could mend and control ma-chinery, that could help a foal or a calf into the world, whose roughness would snag the silk of a party dress.

'I know what's going through your mind.'

Joanna gave Aunt Charly a startled look.

'You're thinking that the refinements seem out of place at Raintree, where the tang off the range blows through the house, and the men seem more at home in boots and spurs than dancing pumps.' Aunt Charly laughed. 'You have expressive eyes, Joanna. They turn you from a quiet girl into a bit of a sorceress. Smoke-blue eyes, like the haze in a summer sky.'

'Now look,' said Joanna, 'we're supposed to be plan-ning the menu for the party sit-down.'

'We'll make ice-cream. There's plenty of vanilla and strawberry essence, and we can add chunks of fruit.'

'You seem more excited about the party than Bonney.'

'Yes, perhaps.' Aunt Charly admired a flower bowl, which was cut like a water-lily with opening petals. 'Girls of today are curiously blasé about the things we enjoyed so much. I think, Joanna, that being young in the old days held a quality of enchantment that is missing from life today – with all its modern improvements. We believed in romance, and we wore the kind of clothes that men liked, and enjoyed being feminine and protected. Tell me, as a girl of today don't you sense there is something missing from your friendships with young men?'

'I haven't any young men.'

'Vance likes you . . . and I think he needs someone like you.'

'Please, Aunt Charly . . .'

'I mean it, Joanna. It would give me a great deal of pleasure to see that handsome devil settle down with a real nice girl. I believe firmly that he has it in him to make a good husband . . .'

'I don't think it would suit Mr. Corraine.'

'You mean Adam?'

'Of course.'

'It's a good strong name to say, yet you never say it.'

'I'm hardly on those sort of terms with him.'

'Nonsense. The Corraines aren't snobs. They don't set themselves up as better than other people because they're successful station-owners, Adam least of all.' Charlotte's eyes sharpened. 'Don't you like him?'

'I think he's a very resourceful and able man.'

'That doesn't answer my question, Joanna. Has Adam said anything to make you feel – unwanted?'

'No – well, he told me in his blunt way not to get any ideas about Vance.'

'He didn't!' Aunt Charly looked amazed.

'He did,' Joanna said with feeling. 'He told me outright that I wasn't the right girl for Vance.'

'Well, I've never known Adam before to interfere in Vance's affairs. Right from boys each has gone his own way with regard to their relaxations and their romances – though Adam always seemed to get more fun out of exploring the rain-forest than the beach at Hawk's Bay.'

This seemed so typical of the man that Joanna had to laugh. 'You're very fond of those two, aren't you, Aunt Charly?'

'They're like the sons I never had, Joanna.'

Joanna was moved by the look in Charlotte's eyes, and she bent forward to kiss the lined cheek that long ago had been smooth as velvet, and tinged with pink to match her party dress as she stood beneath a sparkling chandelier to welcome her guests. So happy, so unaware that her heart was destined to be broken in Queensland.

'What was your party dress like when you were eighteen?' Joanna asked softly.

'It was of pale pink lace trimmed with blue ribbons – my birthday cake was rich with wine and plums. We danced away the hours and I had a cavalier for each dance. I still remember how the brandy punch flared with a blue flame in the big silver bowl.'

'We must have it for Bonney's party,' Joanna suggested. 'In the bowl made from pirate silver.'

Aunt Charly came out of her reverie and gazed for a long silent moment at Joanna. 'I believe you are an exception these days, my dear. I believe you have a romantic heart. Guard it and forget the nonsense I have talked to you about marriage. You will love when you are ready to love, and I hope sincerely, Joanna, that your love is returned by the right man for you.'

Joanna's smile faltered on her lips. 'We've become very serious . . . let's concentrate on the party.'

The morning passed, and the boys had trooped in for lunch, and departed again, when Joanna found the envelope with her name on it, propped against the tea-caddy. Whoever had left it was aware that she always made herself a cup of tea after the bustle of getting the lunches served.

Everything was very quiet as she tore open the envelope and read the note inside – it had been typed on the office machine and some of the letters were tipped with red, like little marks of danger. It was brief and to the point: Miss D. I have to make a flying visit to a neighbour. You might enjoy the trip, which should take a couple of hours there and back. Meet me at the airstrip if you feel inclined. Mr. C.

A smile formed slowly on her lips. She guessed from the way the note was addressed and signed that it was Vance who was inviting her to spend a flying afternoon with him. His hand was healed. The prospect was pleasing. She would wear her cyclamen silk shirt and her best pair of blue jeans . . . and Adam Corraine could think what he liked!

The sky was a hot blue and the tropical trees along the airstrip stood motionless without the stirring of a leaf. Everything looked becalmed. The cattle had sought the shade of the mulgas, and if there were horsemen out on the range they were not visible. It was like a picture in colours of burnt amber, ash-green and burning blue. The air was warm and pungent.

Joanna parked the jeep in the shade of the hangar, and then she walked towards the monoplane, which stood like a big shiny bird on the sandstone runway. Her sun-hat was pulled down rakishly over one eye and her hair was bunched loosely at her nape. Her arms were slim and bare against the pink of her shirt; her jeans were a crisp dark blue and she wore light sandals with a couple of straps.

She could see a tall figure standing beneath the wings of the plane, watching lazily as she crossed the strip towards him, his eyes shaded by a flying-cap with a down-pulled peak. He straightened up as she quickened her pace towards him, and she felt the quick beating of her heart, a sense of strange excitement.

'I see you took time to make yourself beautiful.' The slow and deliberate sweep of the pilot's eyes missed not a detail of her appearance. 'Another five minutes and I'd have been up and away.'

He stepped out from beneath the shadow of the wing, and Joanna caught her breath as she met his gaze. She stood speechless, gazing at the pilot with astonished eyes, wide and smoky beneath her winged brows.

'You?' she exclaimed. 'I thought it was Vance who left me the note to meet him here . . .'

'Did you?' Adam spoke in his softest drawl. 'Do you want to change your mind about flying with me to Monkey Tree Hill?' His lip quirked at her expression. 'Jeff Brennan has them growing about his place. His wife Cherry christened the house Monkey Tree Hill when they moved out from the city five years ago on account of her health. She had a spot of lung trouble, but is entirely better now, thanks to our good air.'

'Well,' Joanna still felt a bit shaken, 'how could I resist such a name for a house?'

'Atta girl!' His smile was quizzical. 'The Brennans have a boy and a girl. Amanda was born out here in Queensland. You'll find her rather cute. I am her godfather.'

He assisted Joanna into the plane, and they buckled

their seat belts. The engine started up and they glided along the runway like a bird. The throbbing of the plane seemed right inside her, or was it her heart still beating madly because this man had fooled her into thinking he was Vance? That note . . . and the physical resemblance . . . he had known even as he stood awaiting her in the shadow of the wings that she would take him for his cousin. She couldn't understand his motive in playing such a game, and she cast him a rather bewildered sideglance.

He was intent on the controls, his profile outlined strongly against the vivid light as they were smoothly airborne and the ground fell rapidly away beneath them. They climbed high over the valley, and Joanna felt the tingle of danger in being so alone with this unpredictable man.

CHAPTER SIX

'Why the masquerade?' she asked impulsively.

'Would you have come on the trip if I had invited you in the usual way?'

'Why should you invite me?'

'Now don't stretch modesty too far,' he mocked.

Her gaze dwelt on his profile and she saw the slash of humour in his cheek. 'The fact is, I want to discuss some business with Jeff and I thought Cherry and her moppet might enjoy your company. You see, Cherry was an English secretary from a place called Leigh-on-Sea. I expect you know it.'

'I do.' Joanna looked at him in amazement. 'Leigh is only a few miles from where I've always lived and I've often been there for a swim, or a meal at one of the seaside restaurants.'

'With a boy-friend?'

'No – after my sister left home it used to get awfully quiet at the week-ends, so I'd take a bus into Leigh and liven myself up with a splash in the sea. It isn't a big, gay place like Hawk's Bay, but quite nice.'

'Good, you and Cherry should find plenty to talk about as you know her home town.'

Joanna studied thoughtfully the far-down view from the cockpit window. 'You knew already – that I used to live only a few miles from Cherry Brennan's home town.'

'I plead guilty to looking it up on an English map.'

'Why do you use the word guilty, Mr. Corraine? Are you hoping I'll feel so homesick that I shall want to go home to Hadley?'

'Now look here—'

She looked and saw that his lips were compressed. 'We get around to a misunderstanding each time we're alone,' he said crisply. 'I was trying to be nice. I'm sorry the impulse misfired.'

'Nice?' For some reason she suddenly began to laugh. Her cheeks warmed and she took off her hat, and at once her hair became the target for the sun. She looked at Adam, who was everything except cosily nice. Even his sun-bitten hands on the controls had a ruthless look about them.

'I don't think you do anything on impulse,' she said. 'You're the most deliberate person I've ever met. You never take aim at a target without meaning to hit it. You like to shape events because you don't like to be shaped by them.'

'You make me sound very arrogant.'

'It is a little arrogant to think you can run other people's lives.'

'Yours and Vance's, do you mean?'

She nodded and kept her gaze averted from his, which she knew would be steel-like and dangerous beneath the flying-cap that emphasized the boldness of his features. 'We're flying over water,' she exclaimed.

A pause, a long one, as they dropped through space and her heart was in her throat. From this height the coral undersea could be seen like a great sinuous snake, seeming to move as the green-blue ocean washed over its spine.

'We're flying over part of the Coral Sea – I thought you'd like to see it,' Adam told her. 'You'll appreciate how many miles separate us from our friends and neighbours in this part of the world. Talking over the radio-telephone is no substitute for a hand-clasp and a face-to-face meeting, and *that* was why I wanted you to meet the Brennans, young lady. Cherry rarely sees another woman, let alone one from her own part of England.'

'You must feel like shaking me.' Joanna gave him a smile that shook him a little. 'But it was a bit of a shock — to find you waiting for me.'

'When you expected to see Vance? You hurried so eagerly – it was a shame to disappoint you.'

'Please – can't we call a truce?'

His grey eyes captured hers for one of those lightning moments. There was a whimsical quality about his smile. 'I'm all for it. The Brennans happen to be my best friends – Jeff used to manage the meat works where I unload my steers – and I don't want Cherry to find out that my rugged charm is lost on my prettiest employee.'

'Don't—' colour flamed in her cheeks, 'don't go to the other extreme, Mr. Corraine.'

'The name is Adam.'

'I – I couldn't.'

'No?' He quirked an eyebrow. 'Can't say my name, and scared I might flirt with you because we're alone in the blue!'

'You're the Boss.'

'Ah yes.' The sky light was in his eyes, making them unreadable, but his smile seemed a trifle mocking. 'A certain formality must be maintained, eh? You're so English, Miss Dowling. Everything about you.'

His eyes flicked her hair and her skin, which was flawless even in the clear sky light in which the plane buzzed like a fly in a saucer of honey. When she looked from the window she saw that the blue-green waves had receded behind them and their winged shadow was passing over burned-gold hills covered here and there with shaggy clusters of sheep.

'Jeff's land,' she was told. 'Now you know who provides those juicy lamb chops we enjoy at Raintree.'

'I thought he was a cattleman like you.' She peered down with interest as they began to descend and a runway ribboned and widened in front of them, and the strap around her waist began to feel tight. She held her breath as the roar of the engine filled the cockpit and their wheels touched down on the tarmac and the air whined past as they ran out of motion. To one side of the strip stood an open-top vehicle. An arm waved, and a hat, and something small in bright pants leapt up and down in the back of the car.

Adam laughed. 'They've come to meet us and they've brought Mandy with them.'

All at once Joanna felt acutely shy. These people were close friends of Adam's, and suddenly it struck her as a most intimate thing that he should bring her to Monkey Tree Hill to meet this family he was so fond of. It glinted in his eyes, a warmth that broke into a smile that held her with its powerful, sudden charm. Like a strong ray of sunlight it burst from its hiding place, and it took away her breath as she followed him out of the plane into the warm golden air and saw him scoop up into his arms the laughing child of Cherry and Jeff Brennan.

'Uncle Dam – ooh, Mamma said you was coming to see us and you came in the plane, didn't you?' She kissed him and snuggled close, batting her eyelashes against his laughter-creased cheek even as she sought about in his pockets with small, eager hands.

'Mandy, now don't be a little fisher.' A young woman came running up to Adam with a wide, welcoming smile under the brim of her linen sunhat. A wave of red hair flopped in her left eye, and her tip-tilted nose and rather thin cheeks were spattered with freckles. 'It's so nice to see you again, Adam. So very nice. And you've brought Bonney – oh, I'm sorry!' Hazel-green eyes dwelt on Joanna with frank surprise and curiosity.

'Mamma, look!' Mandy had found the surprise package she had been searching for.

'Say thank you to Uncle Adam.' Cherry Brennan didn't take her eyes off Joanna as her husband joined the group.

'Son of a gun, how've you been?'

Adam shifted the child to his left arm as he and Jeff Brennan wrung each other's hand. 'Jeff – Cherry, you're both looking great. And I brought a surprise guest with me – someone from your part of the old country, Cherry. Meet Joanna Dowling, who works for us at Raintree. She's a sort of aide-de-camp for Aunt Charly, and before coming out to Australia she lived on the Essex coast.'

'Which part?' Cherry smiled at Joanna, but at the back of her eyes there were question-marks, and Joanna wanted to say outright that she had no designs on Adam Corraine. She knew already that his family and his friends expected him to marry Bonney Ryan.

'Hadley, of all places,' she said, and added lightly, 'Mr. Corraine has told me that you used to live at Leigh, Mrs. Brennan. I knew it well.'

'The Broadway, and the cliffs, and the Ship Inn down where the cockle-boats come drifting in with the tide?' Cherry looked eager, and seemed for a moment to forget her suspicions of Joanna. 'Oh, I did miss that dear old place when I first came to Brisbane to work. I was on the point of running home again when . . . when I met Jeff.' She cast a smile at her husband, who was a lean, brown, soft-spoken man with silver-flecked hair. He carried a battered bush-hat in his hand, and wore a check shirt with khaki trousers.

'How's Terry?' Adam asked, as they made for the car and Mandy sat perched on his shoulder, blowing the toy harmonica he had brought her.

'He was fiddling about with some electrical gadget when we left to come and pick you up.' Jeff grinned. 'I've a feeling, Adam, that my boy isn't cut out for sheep-farming, and I'm not one to press-gang the lad into doing what goes against the grain of him. If he wants something other than sheep-raising, then I shan't stop him.'

'I'll take care of the jumbucks, Dadda.'

'You?' Jeff ruffled his daughter's shining red hair with a fond hand. 'You've always got your ears cocked, like a terrier. Know every word we say, don't you?'

Joanna watched and slowly smiled as the child pressed her bright head against Adam's. 'Uncle Dam brought a lady in the plane, didn't you, big man?'

He laughed outright, deep laughter filled with a warmth that made Joanna view him with new eyes. At Raintree he was always the Boss, busy, practical, riding his range on Blaze, while often at night the desk-lamp shone into the small hours as he pored over a new scheme for his stations.

They climbed into the car, Jeff at the wheel with Adam and the child beside him. Joanna sat at the back with Cherry, while Mandy peered over Adam's shoulder and took her in with impish green eyes.

'Hullo,' she said at last. 'Are you Uncle Dam's lady?'

'Hullo yourself,' Joanna smiled, and hoped Adam was too deep in conversation with his friend to have heard the piping question. 'I work for your uncle and cook nice things for his stockmen.'

'So you come from Essex,' Cherry said again. 'It's just like Adam to spring such a nice surprise on Jeff and me.

We enjoy having visitors, and I haven't had a chance to talk about home in such a long time. How long have you been out here, Joanna? We heard there was a new home-help at Raintree, but I never dreamed you'd be so young. Do you like working for the Corraines?'

It didn't seem to bother Cherry at all that her eager questions could be overheard by Adam, and she looked amused when Joanna gave his broad back a hesitant look.

'Those two are so deep in sheep's wool and cow-hide that woman talk to them is so much wattle fluff on the wind. Tell me all about yourself, Joanna.'

'There isn't all that much to tell—'

'Oh, I was just like you when I first came out.' Cherry laughed. 'Reserved, inclined to think these Aussies a brash and bossy lot. But at heart they're warm and good as the wool they grow – and so tall, don't you think?'

Joanna met the other woman's eyes and she knew that once again Cherry Brennan felt curious about her in relation to Adam. At the plane, with the sun in her eyes, Cherry had assumed upon seeing him with a girl that he had brought Bonney on a visit. Instead he had brought the home-help. An irrepressible laugh broke from Joanna.

'Yes, these men are inclined to be overpowering – Mr. Corraine thought it would be nice for you to meet someone from England who lived so close to your home town. It was only three months ago that I left to come out here – I understand from Mr. Corraine that you've been here for some years, Mrs. Brennan.'

'You must call me Cherry. Well, I met Jeff about six months after I came to Brisbane to work, and our boy is now thirteen. Mandy is just three and a half, aren't you, tinker?'

Mandy gave a fat chuckle and leaned over Adam's shoulder, one hand clasping his brown neck while he continued his conversation with Jeff. 'You're not all brown,' she said to Joanna. 'Only sort of gold.'

A remark which must have penetrated the wool talk up front, for instantly Adam turned his head and his eyes held Joanna. 'How are you girls getting along?' he asked.

'Just fine,' Cherry smiled back at him fondly. 'You know, Adam, you are a surprising man. Why didn't you tell us over the radio-phone that you were bringing an English girl to meet us?'

'Because I'm what you called me – I like to spring surprises on people.'

'Joanna is a very nice one, Adam. When we reach the house and get settled with long cool drinks, she's going to tell me how Leigh is looking after the fourteen years I've been away. Fourteen years! I can hardly believe it's been so long!'

Jeff shot her a smile over his shoulder. 'That's a compliment, Cherry-pie. Shows what a good husband you found for yourself.'

'Australian men don't suffer from modesty, Joanna,' Cherry warned. 'They're well aware that nature made them tall and wide to fit this land. Adam, how is Charlotte these days, and is Bonney as pretty as ever?'

'Prettier,' he drawled, a large hand caressing Mandy's hair, as if the thought of Bonney made him think of the future and a child of his own. 'She'll be eighteen on Saturday and we're giving her a party.'

'Eighteen – already?'

Joanna felt a hazel-green side-glance, and then they arrived at the house on Monkey Tree Hill.

Joanna liked the wide, attractive spread of the house,

with the monkey trees growing on the slopes that cradled it. There was a cool, deep veranda set on wooden pillars, around which flowering vines climbed and clustered. Long cane chairs were set about, with one or two tables, and from the beams of the roof there hung lamps and amusing aborigine carvings.

It was a sun-mellowed house, with the scuffs and marks of children. Toys littered a corner and a rocking-horse snorted as Mandy climbed into the saddle and set it galloping. 'Look at me, Uncle Dam, look at me!'

'Ride 'em, cowboy.'

They stretched out in the cane chairs, and Cherry went to fetch a pitcher of fruit juice, and came back with slices of iced melon as well. Mandy scrambled off the horse and perched on the foot of Joanna's long chair. Soon her face was up to its eyebrows in melon juice, and emerald birds fluttered about the roof of the veranda.

'I still remember how lovely the bells of Leigh Church always sounded on a Sunday, and that part of the cliffs like a hanging garden.' Cherry gave a sad-happy sigh. 'Funny how you look back and the things that seemed a bit dull at the time now take on a sort of long-distance glamour. I worked for an estate-agency and sometimes there was nothing to do but file my nails. My father – he was a widower for several years – married again and being stepdaughter to someone in her thirties was impossible! We couldn't hit it off, and then one day a man came into the agency who had just returned from Australia after thirty years. He was looking for a small house, and we got talking – the upshot was that I fell for the idea of coming Down-Under to work.'

Cherry gazed into her drink, while Mandy looked at her mother with her head cocked. 'Mamma?'

'Eat your melon, darling. I'm enjoying a few memories.'

Cherry smiled. 'I've never regretted coming here, not even when I got rather ill about five years ago and Jeff decided we'd move into the country. It's funny. It's as if every now and again in your life you come to a crossroads and something seems to nudge your shoulder. Did you feel that, Joanna, when you decided to leave home and hearth for the wilds of Queensland?'

'Perhaps.' Joanna felt the impact of grey eyes on her profile. Her head rested against a scarlet cushion, at her feet sat the small lively figure of Mandy. She felt a curious sense of peace, as if for the first time she could relax from feeling guilty about leaving her home and her grandmother, and Gran's equally elderly sister, to strike out for herself in a faraway land.

'Yes, I think I had reached the stage where I was ready to be nudged out of my little hole in the country.'

'Does Queensland frighten you a little, being so big?' Cherry asked. 'I lived in the city with Jeff for nine years, and when we came out here I used to lie awake at night and listen to the strange noises and feel certain I'd never get used to the sheer spaciousness of it all.'

Cherry shot a smile at Adam. 'To a man like Corraine it's his very skin and he loves it, don't you, cobber?'

'It's one of the things I love,' he said in that soft drawl.

Mandy made eyes at him. 'I love you,' she said, sticky-faced and so darned cute that Joanna wanted to hug her close ... close against her heart that was opening wide to this warm land and these people with their rugged warmth.

All at once a boy came strolling round the side of the house. He wore jeans but no shirt. His hair was like burned wheat, and his face was a freckled wedge set with his father's eyes. 'Hi, Adam!' He leapt the veranda steps and broke into a wide smile. 'I heard the plane coming in over the hill, but I was busy fixing the dynamo for the bore of the pool. D'you feel like a swim? The water comes in from deep down and is pretty cool.'

'Would you like to take a swim, Joanna?'

'I'd love it.' She looked from Adam to the boy, who blinked a little with his surprise at seeing a stranger, a girlish one in a cyclamen shirt and blue jeans.

'This is my son Terry,' said Jeff, a note of pride in his voice. 'The pool was his idea, Joanna. He had me and the boys lugging stones and mixing cement for the lining.'

'Joanna.' Terry thrust a hand through his shock of hair. 'That's a nice sort of name.'

'Mandy wants to swim.' The child danced round the chairs. 'I can swim, Uncle Dam.'

'In a rubber belt,' Terry mocked. 'And does she splash, so watch out, everyone.'

Cherry took Joanna to her bedroom to change into a swimsuit, and the two girls had to laugh at the contrast between Joanna's pale skin and Cherry's, which was deeply sun-tanned. 'Being here at Monkey Tree Hill has made me really well again,' she said happily. 'Jeff was awfully worried at the time, and so was I! He was due for a big promotion at the meat-works, and it would have killed me if he hadn't made a go of sheep-farming. Adam has been a marvellous standby. Our first year was a financially bad one, but he saw to it that we didn't go downhill, and through his contacts Jeff found a really good market for his wool.'

Mention of Adam made Joanna feel suddenly shy of being seen by him in the pale gold, one-piece bathing suit. She wouldn't feel half so shy with Vance.

'It's a good thing I hung on to that suit,' said Cherry. 'I've filled out since having Mandy. Oh, for the days when

I had a slim figure like yours! Jeff could span my waist with his hands, almost.'

'You have two fine children,' Joanna said warmly.

'My city boy and my country girl. It's funny, but Terry will want to go to the city to make a career, and Mandy loves the country. You should see her with the new lambs.'

'I can imagine.'

'Adam is very fond of her. She was christened here in the lounge at Monkey Tree. The parson flew from a city church. Some homestead folks are married that way.'

They joined the others at the pool, which was surprisingly attractive with its paved border set with canvas chairs, and trees to shade those who wanted to sun-lounge. Adam was splashing in the water with the two children and their laughter was good to hear. The water caught the inviting sparkle of the sun, and a thrill of pleasure ran through Joanna as she slipped into the pool and swam towards Mandy, who was kicking water all over Adam.

His laughing eyes flashed to meet Joanna's, then a big coloured ball whizzed over from Terry and she ducked, as if it were the ball she avoided rather than the eyes that glinted like crystal against the brown face with water in its crevices and a lance of hair plastered across his forehead. His shoulders were wide and coppery, and dark hair daggered his chest. He looked younger, his cares thrown off those strong shoulders for an hour or two.

They played volley-ball in the pool, and tired at last they joined Cherry and Jeff under the shade trees. Joanna savoured the warm stillness as Mandy fell asleep in the circle of Adam's arm, and she watched the strong repose of his face through her lashes. He cared about the people who were part of Raintree, and he treasured these friends of his, yet she had the feeling that part of him was lonely, as if he had always been too busy to fall in love. Was it possible that pretty, self-centred Bonney could fill the gap in the heart of this man? Perhaps all he wanted now was a son like Terry, and a little girl of his own to sleep with her tousled head against his shoulder.

As the evening sun went down the day grew cool and they went indoors to change out of their swim-suits and to enjoy a cream tea. The lounge grew dim and when Cherry switched on the light it flickered and shone dull in the lamps.

'Something's crook with the generator.' Terry jumped to his feet, wiped cream off his lips with his table napkin, and hurried off to put the matter right.

'It's handy having an electrician in the house,' Jeff grinned. 'Our lighting is operated by a diesel generator. Acts up now and again and Terry fixes it. For my part I'd be happy with kerosene lamps. They're more reliable.'

'Anyone for another cup of tea?' Cherry was standing with the teapot poised in her hand when there was a sudden flash, a dull bang, and everything went dark.

'Terry!'

'The oil-lamps, let's get them alight!' The table shook as Jeff blundered against it, and Joanna felt her heart beat fast with alarm. Mandy began to cry and she reached for the child and held her. 'Hush, poppet. In a minute we'll have some light and will find out what went bang.'

'Went bang,' Mandy echoed, her face pressed against Joanna for comfort.

Jeff got the lamps alight, and Adam took one and they strode out to the veranda and ran down the steps, Cherry following with a frightened look in her eyes. Joanna held on to Mandy and tried not to tremble. The day had been too perfect. Calamity had arrived to cast its shadow – that nice boy with his thatch of wheat-coloured hair had been hurt, the shock of it had penetrated the house from the generator shed.

Adam returned first, carrying the unconscious boy in his arms with great care. Jeff followed with his arm around Cherry, who was weeping. 'Now, now, old girl. He's shocked and a bit burned, but he's breathing. We'll see what's to do, and then I'll get on to the F.D.S. by radio.'

'Jeff, his arm!'

'I know, old dear,' Jeff soothed, while Mandy broke into renewed howls, which Joanna quietened as best she could.

In that strong, silent way of his Adam laid the boy on the sofa and examined carefully the extent of his burns. He turned an expressionless face to Cherry and Jeff. 'We'll just cover these, and I'll fly him straight to the nearest hospital – yes, Cherry! Burns can't be treated here as they should be – now be a good girl and get me the first-aid box. And, Jeff, will you get a couple of blankets to wrap him in.'

'Terry—'

'The sooner we get him some professional help the better he'll be, Cherry,' Adam said practically.

'I ... I know. Adam, he looks so small and hurt, a-and only a little while ago he was eating fruit and cream ...' Cherry crushed a hand against her mouth and hurried into the adjoining room, where something fell and broke as she dragged the medical box out of a cupboard. Joanna met Adam's eyes over the scared child in her arms.

'Cherry will want to fly to the hospital with her boy—'

'Yes.' He stroked the wheaten hair out of the boy's

closed eyes. 'You stay here and look after Mandy. I'll ask Jeff to get through to Raintree by radio-phone to let them know we'll be delayed getting home. Don't look so worried, Joanna. Terry is going to be all right. He's concussed and has some nasty burns on his arm, but it shouldn't take me more than a couple of hours to reach the nearest hospital ... you don't mind staying here? Mandy needs a woman, and you'll be company for Jeff.'

'Of course I'll stay. I'm only sorry that such an enjoyable trip should have ended in this way ...'

'It may be morning before I can get back to you.'

'It doesn't matter, so long as Terry gets the treatment he needs.'

'Crazy kid, so anxious to be a man before he's half out of short pants. Reminds me of myself ... it's something about the country. So much to conquer, so much to take, too little time to play in the yard with childhood things.'

A quarter of an hour later Terry was wrapped in a blanket and carried out to the car. Joanna watched from the veranda as Jeff took the wheel. 'Don't be nervous,' Adam had said to her. 'It won't take Jeff more than a few minutes to drive us to the plane.'

'Safe journey,' she had said to him.

He had looked at her for a long moment. 'You don't flap when there's trouble, do you, Joanna Dowling? I'll see you around sunrise.'

They had gone and everything was quiet again. He had spoken as if he cared about leaving her and would hurry back ... she turned and hurried indoors to Mandy, who had gone to sleep on the sofa in the aftermath of her tears. Joanna bustled about clearing the tea things, as if she needed to keep busy in order to keep her thoughts at bay.

She was at breakfast with Jeff and Mandy when the sound of the homing plane broke the morning silence. 'There's Adam!' Jeff gave her a grateful look. 'You've been a brick, Joanna, staying to look after Mandy and me – now don't worry about the dishes! I'll drive you to the plane right away. Adam said he'd wait there for us.'

Cherry was with him and she ran with a glad cry into Jeff's arms. 'Terry's going to be all right! The doctor reckons he'll be well enough to come home in about a week. They'll bring him in the flying ambulance . . .'

'Mamma, Mandy's here.' The child clamoured to be noticed, and Cherry bent to her and hugged her close. 'How's my big girl? Have you been good while I've been away?'

'Jo-yanna told me a story all about a magic motor car.' Mandy looked around and smiled widely at Adam, who stood tall in the morning sunlight, his eyes holding a lazy smile. 'Where's Terry? Why didn't you bring him back in the plane, Uncle Dam?'

'He hurt his arm, sweetheart, and has to stay in hospital for a little while. He'll be home soon.'

Mandy's eyes grew big and green as she thought this over. 'Did Terry cry when he hurted his arm?' she asked.

'He was very brave, darling.' Cherry pressed a kiss against the little one's bright hair. 'He is in a ward with other children, so he won't miss us too much.'

'All of them hurted, Mamma?'

'Yes, but they're all getting better. Tonight we'll see if we can talk to Terry over the radio-phone, shall we?'

'Yes, Mamma. Oh, I do wish it was tonight!'

As if this underlined the passing of time, Joanna looked at Adam and found him looking at her. 'We'd better be on our way,' he said. 'Say, what have you got in the satchel?'

'There's a flask of tea and some eatables.' Jeff held out his hand to Adam. 'You can enjoy your breakfast in the air, feller. I guessed you'd feel peckish, and saying thanks is not enough.'

'Joanna . . .' Cherry looked at her with eyes still rather puffed and strained. 'You've been so nice about everything . . . what do I say?'

'You said it a few minutes ago,' Joanna smiled. 'Terry is going to be all right.'

After that goodbyes were brisk, as if to cover up feelings laid a little bare by anxiety and its aftermath of relief. From her seat in the plane Joanna waved at the small group down on the strip. Mandy waved back excitedly, a red-haired moppet in sky-blue pants. Joanna felt a lump in her throat. When she left Raintree she would never see again that delightful child, whose, 'Bye-bye, Jo-yanna,' was lost in the roar of the engine as they taxied along the runway for their take-off.

'Bye-bye, little one,' she murmured, and as they lifted into the air she blinked hard to stop her tears from showing.

'I wouldn't mind a cup of tea now we're airborne,' Adam said to her a few minutes later, as they skimmed through a fluffy layer of clouds.

Joanna poured out the tea for him and he drank it thirstily. He enjoyed also a couple of the bacon sandwiches she had made for him back at Monkey Tree Hill. Jeff had put a fruit cake into the satchel as well, also some chocolate and biscuits. 'It's a fair run to Raintree and you might feel like a bite.' She remembered his words, and thought how strong and warm were the ties of these friends who lived so many miles apart.

'Mmm, that feels better,' said Adam. 'Cherry was so

anxious to get back to Jeff and the moppet with the good news about the boy that we didn't stop for breakfast—' There he broke off sharply and when Joanna looked at him, he was staring at the control-panel, his gaze fixed on the fuel gauge.

'Almighty Joe, now I've done it!'

'What is it? What's wrong?' She gave him an anxious look.

'We were thinking so much about Terry – the fact is, Joanna, I forgot to get the plane re-fuelled.' A frown cleft his brows. 'We'll be lucky if we make it as far as Raintree on the fuel we've got left! We could turn back, but that hilly terrain would be dicey to land on if we had to go down in a hurry. I think our best plan is to keep straight on—'

'Won't that mean flying over the sea?' Joanna asked, her pulses set racing by a meeting with Adam's grey eyes.

'We should manage to clear the water, but afterwards I'll take her down on a clear strip of beach. I'm not flying till we run right out of fuel—'

'We'll be stranded!' Joanna gasped.

'We'll be on the right side of the Coral, but it will mean a trek through the forest to Raintree. Sorry this trip is turning into a chapter of accidents, Joanna, but as we say in this part of the world, be prepared for anything. How much tucker did Jeff provide?'

She took a look at the satchel. 'There are a few sandwiches left, a fair-sized cake, a slab of chocolate and some biscuits, nice buttery home-made ones.'

'Good old Jeff!'

'You're being very matter-of-fact about all this,' she protested. 'What about your people – shouldn't you contact them by radio to let them know we're running out of fuel and in for a forced landing?'

'No,' he said quietly. 'Jeff got through to them last night and if we're delayed, they'll think we're still at the Brennans' place and won't worry unduly. If Aunt Charly knew we were in for a forced landing she'd organize a search party, which isn't necessary, and I want those young steers branded. Then there's Bonney . . .'

Of course, Bonney would be bound to worry . . . because Adam was stranded in the rain-forest with another girl, where grew the wild orchids, and where sang the love birds who flew about in pairs. The garden of Eden in which Adam had often roamed . . . this time he would have with him a rather reluctant Eve.

She glanced away from him, and suddenly far below them a shimmer of silvery blue broke through the hazy clouds. 'We're approaching the sea,' she said breathlessly. 'Are you sure we'll make it to the other side?'

Even as she spoke they began to drop down lower, and something about the set of Adam's face told her that already they were losing altitude.

'Whenever I've got to do this,' he said dryly, 'I'll take along a passenger who doesn't flap. Joanna, you're a credit to the British Isles. My father always called the Tommies the best mates on earth to be with in a tight corner.'

After that she had to justify his faith in her, and she sat holding on to her smile, and their satchel of food. The gleaming sea was very close to them now, rippling and winking as the sun touched it, a translucent blue shot with silver, beautiful and dangerous, for fangs of coral lurked under that beguiling surface.

'It's as if the sun has melted sapphires and they've run molten through green woods and brought a tinge of emerald with them.' Joanna spoke her thoughts aloud, but

Adam didn't laugh at her flight of fancy. He glanced at her, at the sun and sea light in her fair hair.

'Do you know what the aborigines say of the sun?'

'No.' She half-smiled and thought them both crazy to be talking of myths and fancies even as the petrol gauge dropped a few points lower.

'They worship the sun as a young goddess; they say she lights up the sea and land with her bright hair and her skirts of gold.'

'That's beautiful,' she said. 'I expect you must have learned a lot from the aborigines.'

'Including bush craft, in case you're worried about getting lost in the woods with me.'

'We're hardly babies,' she murmured.

'I'm not – but in some ways you're pretty innocent.'

'I – I don't understand you.'

'Which proves my point. It might not take too long to fly over a rain-forest, but it takes longer to trek through one.'

She knew at once what he meant. If they landed safely, it would take them some time to reach Raintree. They might have to spend a night alone among the orchids and the raintrees.

Below them now she could see the reef of coral that lay about a mile off-shore. The plane was bumping as the engine grew hungry for fuel. 'Keep your eyes peeled for a likely place where I can bring her down.' Adam was now controlling the monoplane with an effort, for she seemed to be dipping her nose as if at the pull of gravitation. But they couldn't go down anywhere – even as land came into sight and there was a flash of blue and yellow flowers, growing closely together to form a carpet, he said grimly: 'Swamp land. We'd sink like a stone if I went down on to that inviting little patch.'

Joanna gave a shiver, and then her gaze lit on a sand-bar, a creamy-white in the sun patched with the green of palms, jutting out to form a landing strip for them ... if Adam could bring down the plane without too much of a run out, otherwise they'd land in the sea!

'Look!' She caught at his arm and pointed out the sandbar. 'Will it do?'

'You bet your sweet life!'

Now they dropped swiftly and the sea was rushing up to meet them. The engine was whining, and Joanna's heart was in her throat. One slip, one mistake, and she and Adam would be lost together under that white rim of waves breaking around the sandbar. She didn't dare to look at him in case she took his attention off the controls for a single precious moment, but she knew how every line and feature of his face stood out boldly as the sea light flared in on them, and the wheels whipped across the crests of the palm trees and there was a tearing sound as if the bottom of the plane was being ripped away.

'Hold tight!' he rapped at her. 'We're about to get jarred like a couple of bees in a bottle.'

She liked the touch of humour, it braced her as the wheels bounced on the sandbar and they went skidding like mad towards the sea. They roared to their doom, or their salvation, and suddenly there was a lurch and a blinding haze of sand was thrown up as they dipped nose-down in it, only a couple of feet from the water. The plane trembled, then with a thump it settled back and the door was flung wide open.

The wrench of Joanna's safety-belt jarred the breath out of her. As it returned she took a rather stunned look at Adam. Neither of them said anything for several minutes, and there drifted into the plane the smell of seaweed and the sound of the sea washing against the coral underbed of the sandbar. A jagged line of coral could be seen from the cockpit window, and it seemed a miracle that they had stopped short of being ripped to pieces by those sharp teeth.

'Nice timing, Mr. Corraine,' Joanna said with a shaky smile.

'The credit doesn't belong to me.' His eyes held hers. 'That was a stroke of destiny. And now let's see about getting some of the gear to the beach.'

He unhooked his safety-belt, then he leaned forward and she felt his breath stir against her hair as he released her. A smile touched his lips as she let out a sigh of relief.

'I was scared stiff as we came down,' she said, and could feel herself still trembling a little as she looked at him.

'You behaved like a trooper.' He slid from his seat and went to the rear of the tilted plane. 'There should be an emergency box back here.'

He found it, and when opened it revealed some cans of soup, some canned beans, and a tin of coffee. There was also a folded blanket, medications, a box of matches, and a billy-can, which Adam patted as if it were the pet among this precious haul.

'Hand me that satchel,' he said. 'We don't want to cart a heavy box along with us.'

He transferred the tins of food and coffee to the satchel, stuffed the first-aid kit and the matches into his pockets, and handed Joanna the blanket. It was soft as fur and quite large.

'Wallaby lining,' he said. 'Wrapped in a swag like that and you'd sleep as snug as a bug.'

His words sent a ripple of alarm through her. While up in the air it had been easier to face the prospect of being alone at night with him . . . here on the beach, on the edge of the sea, with the forest a mass of green above the sunlit haze of the sands, she was aware of something pagan in the air.

With her every nerve, her every sense, she felt the beat of the waves, the crying of the birds, the tang of coral and seaweed. These were primitive things, and she was alone among them with Adam Corraine.

CHAPTER SEVEN

THEY left the plane and made their way along the sand-bar to the beach. It was around noon and the sun was shining brilliantly on to the sickle of white sand, and the plaited trunks of the palms with down-curving feathery fronds. It was a dream scene, a tropical poster, a place to catch at the imagination and the heart.

But Joanna's heart right now was filled with apprehension of the man who walked tall in the sun at her side. Never had they been so alone in such romantic surroundings. Never before had she been so dependent on another human being, for he alone knew the secrets of the rain-forest and could find the way home through that teeming, shadowy, blossomy jungle.

'We'll rest awhile,' he said. 'Find a shady spot and have some lunch. Are you hungry?'

She stood on the silvery sands and watched the seabirds as they dived on the flying fish, winged arrows along the tips of the waves. Beauty and cruelty . . . holding her as if in a spell.

'Still a bit stunned?'

Fingers gripped her shoulder and she glanced up at Adam. He had discarded his flying-helmet and his hair was ruffled, his collar was open, and his skin was brown as bark. The satchel was flung over his shoulder, and he looked as calm as if they were here on a picnic.

'The plane looks awfully forlorn, stranded out there on the edge of the water. Poor old Bony-bird!'

'Vance's name for the craft.'

'Yes.' She smiled nervously. 'I hope the plane isn't

damaged – he'll be upset.'

'He'd be more upset if anything happened to you – wouldn't he?' Adam's smile was faintly sardonic. 'Now if you'll be a good mate and collect me some pieces of drift-wood – make sure the sun has dried them – I'll get a fire going and we'll have some coffee, and some beans and biscuits. How does that strike you?'

'Right where I'm empty, Mr. Corraine—'

'One minute!'

She had tossed the blanket to the sands and was about to dive off after the driftwood. She looked at him in-quiringly.

'We'll cut out the formalities,' he said. 'This is no place for them. You know my first name so please use it, Joanna.'

'You're the Boss.' She hastened away from him to where the pale sands were patched with pieces of sun-dried wood. She began collecting an armful, and she tried not to think of what might lie behind his statement that this was not the place for keeping up the formalities. For some odd reason she preferred things the way they were between herself and Adam – it was too disturbing when he chose to be less than boss-like. He was somehow not the kind of man you could take in your stride; he made too strong an impact, so that everything he said, or did, took on much more significance.

He might bear a physical resemblance to Vance, but they were not alike in disposition. It wasn't that he had less humour, or less compassion; it was that for Vance life was a plaything, for Adam a vocation.

She brushed a crusting of sand off a piece of wood, and knew that it would have been easier on the feelings to be forced down on the edge of the Coral with Vance.

'Ahoy there!' Adam was calling her from the shade of a

patch of trees, wild banana from the width and raggedness of the leaves that dappled him. 'I want just enough for a cooking fire, not a distress beacon.'

'I'm coming.' She assumed an air of nonchalance as she walked to where he had made camp. She dumped the wood at his feet. It was hot and tendrils of fair hair clung to her forehead beneath the brim of her sunhat. Her cyclamen shirt and blue pants were gay in the sun.

'Can I do anything else to help?' she asked, avoiding the use of his name; avoiding that sense of intimacy it would create to call him Adam.

'No, you cool down while I cook the food.' His brown hands were deft as he laid sticks of wood above the shavings he made with his knife. He shielded a match and lit the shavings, and soon tangy spirals of woodsmoke were drifting upwards, mingling with the sea smells.

Joanna sat beneath the shade of the banana trees with her arms clasped about her updrawn knees. She had tossed off her sunhat because it made her feel warm beneath the shade, and her hair was tousled about the gravity of her face as she watched Adam set the billy-can on the fire, having filled it from the water-bottle. He dug holes in a can of beans and set them to warm at the edge of the fire, and from the satchel he took the butter biscuits. He glanced across at Joanna with a lopsided smile. 'What a pity I can't prove to you how proficient I am with a bent pin and a piece of string. That surf out there is full of fish, and at low tide we could walk to the end of the sandbar and pick mussels and crabs off the coral. What a place, eh? A couple of people could live quite well on the seafood, and the wild bananas when ripe, and the yams that can be dug out of the ground.'

'I don't think it would suit you for long to live in sunlit idleness,' she said, trickling the warm fine sand through her fingers. 'I bet you're impatient right now to get back to the station in case things go slack while you're away.'

'Do you think I'm an all-work and no-play man, Joanna?' He tore off a couple of banana leaves and laid them out as plates. 'You'll have to spoon up your beans with a biscuit, as we're kind of short on cutlery.'

'I think you thrive on work, Mr. ... I mean ... Adam.'

'Don't you care for my name?' He quirked an eyebrow, mocking her hesitation. 'It belongs to a rather intriguing story in the book of books – I'm sure you must have read it.'

'I've read it, but I'm sure there are no serpents lurking on this coral strand, nor are there any apple trees.'

He grinned as he added coffee to the boiling water in the billy and stirred it with a sun-bleached stick of wood. 'This isn't going to taste too tempting without milk – watch the pot for me. There's every chance that I might pick up a coconut. Sometimes they fall or get blown down ... I'm rather on the big side for shinning up a palm tree.'

She smiled and watched him stroll along the beach, his eyes alerted for a coconut palm and a possible windfall. He could be so nice, and it was so disturbing, like a tiger purring in the sun but ready at any moment to show he wasn't tame or predictable. He was lost out of sight around a bend of the beach and she was alone with the bubbling billy, and the roll and thud of the waves, like blue-green swirls of silk unfurling on the sands of crushed coral.

It was a beautiful place and she couldn't help but wonder what it would be like to share it – as if shipwrecked – with a man like Adam. A girl wouldn't starve, nor would she be idle. He was so resourceful that in no time at all they would have built a palm-thatched house and he would have planted yams in their garden, which she would have edged with shells from the beach.

Quite an idyll, if she didn't think too much about other aspects of being a girl entirely alone with a man ... especially when the stars shone through the fronded palms and the sea whispered its seductive music.

Suddenly there was a gleam of white among the undulant palms with the sun in their plumes, and she felt her heart beating in time with the waves as they beat the shore. His fawn trousers were narrow on his hips and his long legs. There was a strong, easy, out-of-doors swing to his way of walking. Much of the time at Raintree she had seen him on horseback and it seemed a little strange to see him out of the saddle.

'We're in luck.' He carried two large tufted coconuts. 'There's even a dairy on this golden strand.'

'No boutiques, no beauty parlour?' she asked daringly.

His eyes captured hers and strong between them for a moment was the memory of their first meeting. He had not spared her, because right away he had taken her for Vance's girl. The kind of girl who thought of nothing but making herself attractive rather than useful.

He shrugged his shoulders and looked curiously pained, as if he had hoped she'd forgotten, or forgiven him for the things he had said that day. 'You'll never know how you looked,' he said, 'standing there under the Australian sun, all daisy fresh, plucked out of an English garden, and certain sure to wilt within a week. Now I had all those steak lunches in mind—'

He laughed, gave a groan. 'No use thinking about steak right now. Let's get these nuts cracked and we'll have milk in our coffee.'

He found a stone and after a bit of battering the shell yielded and Joanna held the nut while he lifted the billy from the fire with a stick under the handle and poured out the coffee, using the cups off the flask and the water-bottle. He added a little of the coconut milk to each cup and they quenched their thirst in silent bliss. Afterwards he dished up the beans and they sat propped against the banana trees and enjoyed their lunch, finishing up with a slice of fruit cake each.

'Not bad food for a marooned couple,' Adam said lazily. 'More coffee, or are you replete?'

'Just half a cup, please.'

'You look comfortable,' He flicked his eyes over her slim, relaxed figure, tucked into the incline of a tropical tree. 'As if you belong to a coral beach ... a sort of mermaid in blue jeans.'

She sipped her coffee, sunwarmed, at peace, yet aware of the need to know when he meant to start the homeward trek. She looked at him, the question in her eyes.

'Are you so anxious to leave all this?' The look he gave her was faintly teasing. 'Are you scared we'll be alone in the rain-forest at nightfall? I'm afraid we will, Joanna, whether we leave now or rest for an hour. I'd advise you to rest, because the going through the forest won't be all that easy. It's a wild place, teeming with vines and vegetation, not to mention insects, moths and fruit bats.'

'Sounds as if I'm going to enjoy myself!'

'Have you got one of those filmy handkerchiefs with you? My tough skin can take scratches and bites, but from the look of yours—' Again that flash of lightning grey over her slim neck and bare arms. 'A chiffon square would offer some protection – in fact, when we get going you'd better wear my flying-jacket. It's of canvas and not overwarm. Those arms of yours will be made a meal of if they aren't protected.'

His concern was confusing, and she bent her head to search her shoulder-strap bag, which was of soft leather that stretched to accommodate a number of things a woman found handy to have with her on a trip. She sorted around in her bag, but knew in advance that she wasn't carrying a chiffon square. Bonney Ryan was the girl for a flutter of chiffon at her throat or around her hair.

'What have you got in there?' Adam peered forward to have a look. 'Any cigarettes?'

'Sorry, I don't smoke. I've some mints if you'd like a chew.'

'I won't say no.' He accepted a couple and crunched away contentedly, the peak of his flying-cap shielding his eyes from the dazzle of the sea. His long legs were stretched out, and his left hand played idly with the soft sand.

'Relax for a while,' he said. 'You can wear my jacket and look helpless and cute in it.'

'I can remember the day, Mr. Corraine—'

'Now none of that, Joanna Dowling.'

She looked at him suspiciously, for he seemed to make her name sound like Darling on purpose. She couldn't see his eyes, but his lips were quirked ... firm, well-cut lips blending with the strength of that square-cut chin. A shaft of gold through the trees lit upon his brown throat. She was very aware of him beside her, and of the seductive lisp of the sea, the sensuous warmth of the sun, the wild beauty of it all.

She rested against the tufted tree, her toes in the warm white sand, pleasantly tickling. She was almost on the verge of slumber when Adam startled her by surging to his feet and lifting her bodily a yard or so from their resting place. 'W—what are you doing?' she stammered, feeling the hard crush of his arms and then their abrupt release.

'Saltbush snake!' He flung the words over his shoulder, and she watched dumbly as he swung a rock and crushed something against the trunk of the tree where she had been dozing. A hand crept to her throat. No snakes, she had said, and all the time that slim and dangerous thing had been slithering nearer and nearer, until Adam's quick eyes had spotted it and with equal alertness he had swung her out of its reach.

She swallowed dryly. 'Another minute—'

'Yes,' he said laconically, and he began to check their gear. 'Snakes travel in pairs ...' He shook the wallaby rug, prodded about in the satchel, and even took a look inside her sandals, which she had slipped off so she could feel the softness of the sand with her feet. Now she became aware of their vulnerability and she ran towards him, holding out her hand for her sandals.

'Come on, I'll latch them for you.'

She put a hand on his shoulder to steady herself and felt the hard bone and sinew of him. 'Ooh!' she half-laughed as his hard fingers scratched against her instep. 'Thank you ... for what you did ... Adam.'

'I wonder what would have happened if my namesake had dispatched that other serpent in the garden?' He looked at her and his eyes were crystalline and amused. 'Any theories?'

'I don't reckon we'd be here, do you? If the story is fact and not fiction?'

He laughed and she felt his arm twine lazily about her waist as they stood and gazed out towards the sandbar, where the plane was abandoned, one side tilted downwards like a bird with a bent wing.

'What will you do about the plane?' She stood tense within the circle of his arm, and she was intensely aware that her head came only as high as his shoulder. It had been awkward for him to get his lean length in and out of that cockpit, looking so tiny from here.

'When we reach Raintree I'll get in touch with a shore station and have them refuel her and fly her home. Her undercarriage is a mite damaged, but she'll make it home.'

'Adam ...?'

He looked down at her, and she was shot through with disorganized feelings about him. Why this wariness in his presence; this tenseness at a touch that was merely protective? It was as if she were afraid of liking him, and never for a moment had she felt any doubt about liking Vance.

'What if the folks at Raintree get in touch with Jeff Brennan by radio and he tells them we left Monkey Hill soon after breakfast? Won't they be terribly worried?'

'What would you have me do?' He looked quizzical. 'We're well and safe, a little worrying won't hurt them, and we'll be home by tomorrow.'

'Couldn't we go out to the plane and contact them by radio? They might think we've had a crash ...'

Even as she spoke the breakers crashed over the sand-bar, sending white fangs of spray into the air, and she heard Adam laugh drily above her head.

'I could swim out,' he drawled, 'but this is probably a shark bay.'

'Sharks?' she gasped.

'These waters are alive with them, and it's handy to have a pair of legs for a trek through the rain-forest.'

He grinned, and then she felt the sudden tightening of his arm as she shivered. She went cold all through, and he let her go, picked up his flying-jacket, shook it hard, and then draped it around her shoulders.

'You weren't to know about the sharks,' he teased. 'And I know you're worried about Aunt Charly – and the others.'

She caught the note of meaning in his voice; he meant Vance and what his cousin's reaction would be to this jaunt which had led to a forced landing. Then there was Bonney . . . how would she react to Adam spending a day and a night alone with another girl? And what would the people of the valley have to say when they heard that the English girl had been involved in an adventure with the Boss?

There was no reading Adam's face for the answer. Looking calm and controlled he set about rolling their gear in the wallaby rug, so that it resembled the swags the stockmen carried on their saddles when they set out for night duty on the range. 'There's a length of string in the left pocket of my jacket,' he said. 'Will you toss it to me so I can make a shoulder sling for the gear.'

'I'd like to carry something,' she offered.

'I've a broad pair of shoulders, Joanna,' his smile was whimsical, 'and I'm used to toting a swag.'

'All right, be independent,' she half-smiled, and sorted around in his pockets for the coil of string. She handed it to him and watched as he plaited it to make it stronger, then he tied the ends of the rug, in which everything was neatly rolled, and made a broad loop to pass over his shoulder.

'Are we ready?' He looked her over. 'Y'know, it might be better if you tuck your hair under your hat, or braid it. You don't want moths flying into that golden net.'

Her cheeks warmed and she told herself it was the sun on her face. 'I'll make a braid,' she said, and with fingers a little clumsier than usual – because never before had she been watched by a man as she did her hair – she divided the soft strands and plaited them. She fixed the end with a scrap of ribbon found in her bag, and the braid hung down over her shoulder, beneath her sunhat, and she knew she looked amusing from the glint in Adam's eyes.

'Now I know how you looked when you went to school,' he said. 'Come on, pigtail, let's be moving – but first have you got everything? I noticed you were carrying everything but a vase of flowers in that bag of yours.'

'Really, you men haven't a bit of gallantry these days,' she said, as they began the climb up the sloping beach to the entangled greenery of the forest. 'You don't allow us to have any more mystery.'

'On the contrary, I happen to think certain women as mysterious as this rain-forest. A man can feel a mite unsure of himself, until he gets his bearings and begins to untangle some of her ways.'

'I can't imagine you ever being unsure of yourself, not in a forest, or with a woman.' She skipped under the vinery he held aloft for her. 'Well, not since you were a boy.'

'You've heard some of the tales, eh, about how King Corraine took me in hand and laid a whip across my shoulders for having a will of my own?'

'Vance did mention the incident—'

'You and Vance appear to have talked often about the history of Raintree.'

'No – Aunt Charly has told me one or two stories about your ancestors, and your antics as boys.'

'Really?' He shot a grin down at her, a green and gold

shadow across his face, the peak of his cap turned up, his eyes amused and inquiring. 'What did she tell you?'

'Oh, that Vance liked the gaiety of Hawk's Bay, while you liked to explore the valley and the rain forest.'

'True. Vance always was the one for smooth things, while I liked the going to be a bit more rugged. We're not very alike, Joanna.'

'There are times when you look alike,' she said impulsively.

He laughed, startling a trio of birds out of a bush, their plumage as bright as petals in the shafts of sunlight through the towering trees. 'We're both chips off our grandfather, but I came off the rugged side of King Corraine.

For some reason his words touched Joanna. Adam must often have rebelled as a boy against the demands made on him by King to be a man, a boss, a leader of other men ... while Vance was left free to enjoy the privilege of being a Corraine of Raintree Valley. The handsome, charming member of the clan, who had no need to be tough, shrewd and self-sufficient because the running of Raintree and the other stations would not be his responsibility.

She wanted to tell Adam that she understood his feelings, because in a similar sort of way her own adolescence had been more work than play.

She gave him a questing look, but his attention was upon the path ahead of them. It was becoming more overgrown, dim with shadows, alive with hummings, and a profusion of snaking, tangled, many-hued vines. Ropes and ribbons and sudden traps, catching at the foot, or an arm, like live things. There were trees that spread their roots for yards on end, sun and rain-mottled giants that reared into the sky and spread a great parasol of green-tinged shade. Despite this shade it was warm; an earthy, moist kind of warmth that made Joanna's shirt cling to her skin; that encouraged into growth the cascades of orange-coloured trumpets that grew down the trunks of the forest trees, and which expelled a musky perfume when Adam brushed them aside.

As the going grew more tiring, and the scents and the warmth more languorous, Joanna began to have that heady sense of unreality which is usually aroused by a glass of rich wine. She was half bemused, half fascinated, and wholly at the mercy of Adam and his forest lore. If he took a wrong turning she would follow and they would both be lost in the wild heart of the forest, and somehow that would be more dangerous than anything else. Everything here was so untamed, with flowers burning like flame in the shafts of green-gold sunlight.

When Adam turned to make sure that she wasn't getting tangled up, that strange green-gold light struck across his face and its strong planes and angles, lit by the glint of his eyes.

'Are you all right?' he asked. 'Not getting tired?'

The ground was uneven, and a couple of times she had almost been tripped by ropy vines. Her ankles ached, and the cloying heat seemed to press against her temples, but she said doggedly that she was okay and they pressed on through the maze of creepers, waist-high ferns, and great velvety leaves that wagged like ears as they brushed past them.

Insects buzzed, and there were alarming sudden squawks in the bushes. A glinting mantis would hover in a coppery sun-shaft, or a winged creature would fly out from a clump of ginger and brush itself against Joanna as if curious, or attracted by her hair or the cyclamen pink of her shirt.

It was – despite her tiredness – a world of wonder. A forest of Arden. *Under the greenwood tree, who loves to lie with me* ...

Lost in her thoughts she didn't watch her step and the next moment her foot caught in a vine and she went sprawling. Luckily she landed in a patch of those velvety leaves, and it was Adam who swung her upright with his easy strength.

'You're getting weary,' he said, and his hands still held her, warm about her slim bare arms, 'and soon it will be dark – here in the forest the darkness comes quickly. We'll find a place to camp ...'

'Adam ...' her heart was beating quickly from her headlong fall, 'I can go on for another hour or so.'

'I think not,' he said decisively. 'I don't want a worn-out girl on my hands. For the last ten minutes we've been heading in the direction of water ...'

'How can you tell?' she broke in.

'From the calls of the birds. Listen, can't you hear them whistling and twittering just ahead of us? Dusk is coming on and they're congregating near running water.'

She and Adam stood very still for a moment, and she heard the piping whistles in the trees, and the beat of her heart. She glanced up at Adam and found him looking at her. A tousled lock of hair fell across his forehead and he looked every inch the son of pioneers; a man with a love of the wilds running in his veins. His tanned skin was agleam with perspiration, and his shirt was thrown wide open at his muscular throat. There was a power and a passion in him that the forest drew forth, just as it drew wild scents from the raintrees.

'You look a little frightened,' he said, and he half-smiled down into her eyes, smoke-blue shadows in her slender face. 'I shan't lead you astray, Joanna.'

Her reaction to his words, and his closeness, was a primitive rush of confusion, so overwhelming that she had to break free of his touch.

She pulled sharply away from him, and at once his smile was gone and a frown darkened his eyes. 'Women always assume that a man deals in double talk,' he said crisply. 'Are you afraid in case I kiss you?'

'Do you imagine I'd let you, without putting up a fight?' she retorted.

'Battling words, Joanna,' he mocked. 'Maybe if I kissed you here and now it might make things easier between us when we have to bed down for the night.'

'Wh-what do you mean?' she gasped.

'Well,' he drawled, 'you're all on edge right now, wondering when I'm going to pounce, so let's get it over and done with.'

He came a step nearer and she backed away from his mocking eyes, his wide shoulders and powerful arms. 'Please, stop it!'

'You started it.'

'I – I did nothing of the sort!'

'Now, now, Joanna, you took my chivalrous intentions for the other sort. Wasn't that why you jumped a yard away from me a moment ago?'

'I – I thought it time we moved on,' she said desperately. 'I'm terribly thirsty.'

'You prefer coffee to a kiss?'

'Please, Adam, don't be mean.'

He studied her, pressed against a raintree with a chain of scarlet creepers holding her. The green shadows across his face made him look devilish, and a tremor ran through her and she didn't know why it was so imperative that he didn't kiss her . . . just to be tormenting.

'I'm not mean, Joanna, I'm like every other man. Only

like everyone else you think I've got to act the stony image of a boss all the time, in any situation. Didn't it occur to you that I was darn worried about bringing that plane down? We could so easily have crashed on the coral reef and I didn't want to be responsible for hurting you, or killing you. I'm not made of stone. A kiss from me wouldn't leave you with a bruise!'

'Why should you want to – to kiss me?' She could speak only in a whisper, for once again this enigmatical man had moved her, shaken her.

'Just to feel you alive, just to know I didn't break you in two out on that reef.' His smile was a mixture of irony and whimsy. 'Vance wouldn't have hesitated, back there on the beach, but that would have been a different story, eh?'

He hitched the swag that hung at an angle across his back, the loop of string pressing deep into his shoulder. 'Come on, porcupine, give your prickles a rest and let's be finding that camp site before it gets dark ... as I said, night falls quickly here in the rain-forest.'

The creeper-hung trees made a canopy over the small clearing where Adam dropped the swag and stretched his arms with a deep groan of relief. Joanna stood gazing breathlessly at the willow-like trees that dripped their tresses into the stream that ran like a strip of silver through the forest. The birds for a moment had gone silent, as if peering in sharp-eyed curiosity from the branches overhead. Wings flapped nervously as Joanna swung round to Adam with the light from the stream shining in her eyes.

'I'm hot and sticky, my feet ache, and I'd love nothing better than a cool, cool dip in all that lovely water. May I, Adam? Would it be all right?'

'Certainly, but I don't know what you're going to use

for a towel. I won't let you drip-dry. You might catch a chill.'

'Oh, I must take a bath! I can't bear to feel grubby a moment longer. Jeff wrapped the sandwiches and the cake in a tea-towel – couldn't I use that to rub myself down?'

'If you don't mind a few crumbs.' She had the impression that he was grinning slightly as he unrolled the wallaby rug and produced the satchel of food. 'What if I decide to join you?'

'Oh—' She caught her breath. 'Couldn't you wait till I come out?'

'I guess I shall have to. In any case a tea-towel wouldn't be much use for mopping my bulk dry.' He handed her the towel and she caught the glint of amusement in his eyes. 'I'll get a fire going and the billy will be bubbling with hot coffee by the time you've had your dip. These forest streams run cool and clear, so you won't be disturbed.'

He walked with her to the edge of the stream, where he filled the billy-can. Now the forest birds had begun to twitter and call again, sweet long sounds echoing through the green mazes of the forest, and Joanna smiled involuntarily, for somehow the presence of the birds made her aloneness with Adam less acute. Their tiff among the scarlet creepers had left a residue of tension, so that each time their eyes met, each time they spoke, it was as if a fine wire shimmered between them.

If she provoked him now . . . if he touched her now . . . there would be fireworks.

'Call out if anything alarms you,' he said. 'The flying foxes have rather large wings, but they're harmless, unless you happen to be growing on a tree.'

Before he left her to bathe in the stream he took a look

among the willow-like trees. The light was fast fading, but still the stream held a hint of silver and it outlined him tall and dark as he turned to her. 'There's no turkey-bush for you to get scratched on.' His teeth glimmered in a smile. 'Enjoy your dip.'

She watched him disappear among the trees, and as she unbuckled the belt of her jeans a peewee cried across the stream, a long and rather lonely sound, as if the bird were calling home its mate to their resting place. There was a strong scent of nectar, stealing out from the grevillea that grew wild, and the tree-orchids that were rich in perfume. The water shimmered as Joanna slipped into it, and she wondered with a little shiver of pleasure and coldness what Gran would say, what Viviana would think if they could see her now, bathing like this – a nymph in a forest stream – with a man of the Australian range only a few yards away. He was hidden by the trees, and busy building a fire for their supper of soup and biscuits, but she was very aware of him as she splashed about in the stream and felt a tingling aliveness from her toes to the tips of her ears.

She tried to picture the Joanna she had been, travelling out sedately from England to join her sister, but the outlines blurred and she knew that some intrinsic change had taken place and she not only felt different, she looked less serious and reserved.

She laughed to herself. In the old days she would not have dreamed of swimming without a stitch of clothing.

CHAPTER EIGHT

WHEN Joanna pulled herself out of the water the night had grown a little colder and she rubbed down briskly with the rather inadequate towel and was glad to slip into her clothes. The ends of her hair were damp and she looked forward to warming herself beside the fire, whose tangy smoke stole among the trees along with the aroma of coffee. She stepped into her sandals and was latching them when a harsh cry rang out from among the bushes, abruptly broken off, leaving a silence filled with the hammering of her heart.

For a second or two she couldn't move, only her lips moved, murmuring a name.

'*Adam* ...' She broke into a run, thrusting her way towards the ruddy glow of the fire, where the billy boiled merrily with the coffee in it.

'Adam – where are you?'

'Here, Joanna.'

She swung round, white-faced, as he emerged from the bushes carrying something in his hand.

'What – what was that awful cry?' she gasped.

'It wasn't me, honey.' The casual endearment shook the ground again and she didn't know whether to weep with relief because he was all right, or to stamp her foot at his exasperating calmness.

'I – I thought you were being murdered.'

'Well, you could say something like it was going on.' He held aloft the object in his hand, feathered, with a long, scrawny, broken neck. Adam's mouth crooked into a grin. 'I heard him grubbing about in the bushes and stalked him – one quick grab and we have turkey to go with our soup. It should taste fine roasted in the hot wood ashes.'

'Well,' Joanna's smile trembled on her lips, 'he sounded very reluctant to provide us with supper, and he looks a bit scrawny.'

'Now that's just like a woman,' Adam mocked, 'after I bring food to the hearth like a regular cave-man!'

She laughed, but as they walked to the fireplace, which Adam had built within a ring of stones, she felt a trembling in her legs. Her fear had been for him, not for herself. And she knew, with the force of a blow, that if anything should ever happen to this big, able, strangely protective man, it would take the sun and the stars out of the sky for her.

As she looked at him, at his face bronzed by the firelight, she knew that slowly, inexorably, Adam Corraine had walked into her heart, and her heart had enclosed him and there he would remain, even when a thousand miles separated them.

He lifted the billy-can from the fire with a stick of wood under the handle and settled it on a stone. He then put more wood on the fire, so that when it burnt down there would be a bed of ashes in which to roast the scrub-turkey, and his brown hands moved deftly, etched by the firelight, as he plucked and cleaned the bird. A breeze rustled through the trees, stirring the woodsmoke, and Joanna zipped his flying-jacket to her throat with a tingling sense of pleasure in wearing a garment of his.

While the bird roasted in the glowing ashes, they sat on a log and enjoyed their coffee, and there danced about them lovely plushy moths with wings of silk painted with golden eyes. The soft pulsing of the wings, and the forest murmurings, bathed Joanna in a cool peace after the turbulent discovery that she was in love with Adam. She hugged her secret, as she hugged her cup of coffee, and didn't think beyond these hours with him. Tomorrow she would have to face reality, but right now it was good to dream. All this she would have to remember when she left Raintree ... to stay and see him marry another girl was not possible.

'You seem far away in your thoughts,' he said, as he turned the baking bird with a pronged stick. 'A penny for them?'

'Oh, I was just thinking that we should arrive home in time for Bonney's party. She'll be very disappointed if you're not there when she blows out the candles on her cake and unwraps her presents.'

'I wouldn't want to disappoint Bonney,' he agreed. 'It was only a couple of years ago that she lost everything, and we try to make up for that, Aunt Charly and I.'

Joanna caught the compassionate note in his voice, and she kept her gaze on a filmy-winged moth, which seemed to hover dangerously close to the flames of the fire. 'The foolish thing will burn itself in a moment,' she whispered.

'Evidently a female of the species,' he drawled. 'Tempting danger and ending up with singed wings.'

Again and again the moth vibrated about their fire, bringing Joanna's heart into her throat in case it scorched those shimmering wings. Then all at once it glided off among the dark trees as if aware that ecstasy could end only in pain.

'Relieved?' he murmured. 'In case even that small thing should hurt itself?'

'It was so lovely.'

He was silent and she felt compelled to look at him. Her eyes in the firelight held a blue sorcery. The shadows played in the young hollows of her face. She was defenceless in her love, but hiding it with a proud tilt to her chin. She was fragile in his flying-jacket, and yet not helpless or unhurt by the realities of life. Her hair was a soft rope of gold against the brown canvas jacket.

The firelight was in his eyes as he looked at her and she could not read their expression. 'You're very appealing in my jacket,' he said, and then he gave a laugh. 'Now don't get all starched up because I pay you a bit of flattery. Right now I'm hungry for a turkey leg, so you're quite safe.'

'Will supper soon be ready?' she asked, an ache in her throat because she had to resist his teasing. Even the brush of his arm sent a tingle of awareness through her, and she hated shrinking from him when she longed to sit close to his warm strength.

'We might as well have our soup.' She felt him looking at her with a slight frown as he poured the soup into the cups, hot and spiced. 'Here you are, Joanna.'

'Thank you.' Her fingers brushed his as she took the cup. 'It smells good.'

'Ever camped out like this before?'

'Only with the girl guides,' she smiled.

'H'm, that would be a trifle different from sharing meals and a camp fire with a man.' The smile he gave her was a trifle wicked. 'Do you write and tell your grandmother all about your new life in Queensland?'

'I tell her the things that won't worry her – and you're forgetting that I'm only a working visitor. I haven't planned to settle here for good.'

'You mean to return to England after you've seen your sister?'

'I – I probably shall.'

'Suppose someone tried to stop you?'

She looked at him quickly. 'I never took Vance's proposal seriously, if you're referring to him. And didn't you say that you'd do your darnedest to stop him from marrying me?'

'My very darnedest,' he agreed, his voice a low thunder by the warm red glow of the fire. 'I'd sooner see you go back to the old country than see you married to my cousin.'

'You don't beat about the bush, do you?' And because she loved him, hurt anger flared that he should be so open about not wanting her to become a Corraine. A tremor shook her. She wanted to raise her hand and feel his hard jaw beneath a stinging slap. How dared he talk about wanting to kiss her when he didn't think her good enough for Vance! Her cheeks burned and she jumped to her feet.

'You're the most arrogant devil it's ever been my misfortune to meet,' she said hotly. 'You live in a world of your own, a bossy autocrat who actually goes pale at the thought of a kitchen wench marrying into the clan Corraine! Watch out, Adam! You're on the way to becoming as hard as your grandfather, and from all accounts his wife pined away from lack of love.'

Adam stared at her, and then in a voice dangerously quiet he said, 'Sit down, Joanna. Your nerves are all on edge, otherwise I'd be angry with you for saying those things.'

'They're true, aren't they? The truth always hurts.'

'Are you trying to make me angry, Joanna?'

She didn't answer him, but the tilt of her chin was defiant.

'Now sit down,' he ordered. 'I'm about to dish up the turkey and we don't want a quarrel to upset our digestions. See, it's baked to a turn.' With the aid of the pronged stick he transferred the smoking bird from the bed of hot ashes to a platter of leaves and using his knife he scraped off the ash and carved off the legs. Then he looked at Joanna and she knew from the flash in his eyes that if she didn't rejoin him on the log he would take hold of her and make her sit beside him. If he touched her, after the things she had said to him, she might do something foolish. She might bury her head against his shoulder and whisper that she didn't care if he was arrogant. She loved him despite everything. His strong profile etched by the firelight. His wide shoulders. The way he had of being in command of every situation.

She sat down and meekly took the leg of turkey which he handed to her on one of those handy green leaves. 'You're hungry,' he said. 'You'll feel less jumpy once you've had something substantial to eat.'

She blinked as she nibbled her turkey leg and told herself there was smoke in her eyes.

'Good?' he asked, after taking the edge off his hunger.

She nodded. 'It's much nicer than biscuits.'

His teeth glimmered. 'I'm glad I make a satisfactory chef.'

'You're never at the mercy of any situation.' The turkey meat was crisp and tasty. 'If I were alone I'd still be struggling to light a fire, probably with green wood, and I'd be scared of all those eerie noises among the trees.'

'A man has to be self-sufficient, Joanna. This is a big land.'

'I don't like to think how big,' she murmured, and she was thinking of the many miles that would one day separate them, and when like Charlotte Corraine she would love forever the memory of a man who was unlike

163

other men. His face would haunt her, for it was carved so boldly and strongly. And his voice would be a low thunder in her ears . . . when others spoke her name she would remember how it sounded on his lips.

The flames of their fire leapt warm, but beyond lay the blackness of the forest, filled with croakings and stealthy rustlings.

'Don't you like Australia?' he asked suddenly.

She thought of Raintree Valley, which she had grown to love. She pictured all the rest, the vast outback, the stretches of bush, the great cities, and she felt small and lost. This was in her eyes, reflected there for him to see. 'I guess New Zealand will suit you best.' There was a note of impatience in his voice. 'It's smaller, prettier, and full of woolly lambs.'

'Don't—' She reached out a hand to him, and then hastily withdrew it. 'You were born here, Adam. You're big yourself, so its vastness can't frighten you. You have your family, your friends—'

'You want to be with your sister, is that it?'

'We're twins and it's been such a long time since I saw Viv. She's so gay and sparkling, and she treats life like an amusing game. I'm the serious one.'

'You'll have plenty to tell your sister.' He leaned forward to replenish the fire with a branch of wood that burned blue as it took flame and sent a whiff of incense into the air. Fireflies were sparks in the darkness beyond the rim of leaping firelight. As he leaned back on the log Adam whistled a few bars of *Waltzing Matilda*.

'This kind of thing wouldn't appeal to Viv.' Joanna smiled as she watched the dance of many tiny moths in the glow of the fire. 'She likes the glamour of rustly dresses and restaurants. . . if she were here right now she'd be on the lookout for creepy crawlies, and she'd expect chestnut stuffing with the turkey and table napkins. I'm afraid you'd never take my twin for a country girl.'

He laughed quietly, that pleasant baritone sound that played its way to her heart and made loving him no easy thing to bear in silence and secrecy.

'It's funny,' he said. 'I can't imagine a replica of you, Joanna. Your eyes, that spirited tilt to your chin, and the golden rain of your hair, they seem to belong only to you. I can't picture another girl with quite your look.'

'Oh, everything about me is quiet compared to the dazzle Viv creates when she walks into a room. We're not strikingly alike ... though we're twins. Viviana is beautiful.'

'Is that supposed to be everything?' he drawled.

'Not here, I suppose, in the wilds of Queensland,' Joanna smiled. 'I wonder what you'd have said if Viv had turned up at Raintree for the job of home-help?'

'I'd have sent her packing for certain sure,' he grinned. 'If she's as decorative as you say, then those stockmen of mine would have camped on the kitchen doorstep. As it was, young lady ...'

She looked at him as he paused significantly, and there rushed over her the memory of his hostility. The way he had sat his horse in the sunlight and swept his eyes over her. He hadn't thought then that she had spirit. It had irritated him that she should be clad in Vance's flying-jacket. He had looked all set to bundle her back on the plane with a reject label around her neck.

'You couldn't stand me,' she laughed, and there was a catch in her throat. 'I wanted to tell you to keep your job.'

'Joanna—' He sat forward, the glimmer of the firelight on his white shirt, his brown face, his eyes etched by sun-lines and those caused by the many cares of being the Boss.

'It's all right. I understand now,' she said, her hands dug deep into the pockets of his jacket; hands that longed to smooth the lines in his face.

'What do you understand?' he asked swiftly.

'That you had the best interests of Raintree at heart, and you thought I'd be a liability.' She tilted her chin and gave him a steady look. 'I proved you wrong. I bet not many people have done that to Adam Corraine.'

'No.' His eyes held hers. 'The boss of a station can't afford to be a duffer, but let's set the record straight about something—'

Whatever it was he was going to say was interrupted by a sudden fluttering in the shadows. The thing swooped, with a wide spread of wings, and Joanna jumped up, alarmed, as it dived towards them.

'It's all right!' Adam gripped her within the circle of his arm and swung her to him, her face pressed to his shoulder. The night creature winged around them and then dived off as Adam flung a piece of firewood.

'What was it?' she gasped, pulling away from him.

'A flying-fox. They make a peculiar noise, don't they? It was probably attracted by the smell of our food ... Joanna, you're shaking!'

It was reaction from his closeness, the joy of it, and the denial of that joy. 'I'm as bad as Viv and her creepy-crawlies.' She forced herself to laugh. 'We'd better clear away the supper things. I don't fancy seeing that vampire again.'

'Yes, let's get the dishes washed,' he said briskly.

They went down to the stream to wash the billy-can and the cups and she was glad when he said he'd postpone his dip until the morning. It was so late now, and the rain-forest was so mysterious, unlit by the stars that shone in the patch of velvety sky above the stream. The water rippled, the trees rustled as a wind stirred their long hanging leaves, and she felt the spell of the night, which the presence of Adam made safe for her ... and at the same time dangerous.

He stripped off his shirt and splashed the cool water over his face, throat and shoulders. He flicked his hair back, dark with water, and there in the starlight his wet torso was silvery. She tossed him the towel they had dried by the fire and he used it vigorously, a big, warm, healthy male creature who was at one with the elemental things.

'That was good.' He buttoned his shirt, and they made their way back to the camp fire. Something was nosing around the satchel, but it scampered off as they appeared. 'A forest cat,' he said. 'They prowl about but don't stay to argue – I'll make up the fire and that should keep off the intruders.'

He shot her a look as the flames leapt around the firewood. 'Afraid of the bush at night?'

She considered his question, a slender figure in the firelight, hands buried in the pockets of his jacket, the collar turned up about her slim neck. 'You're here,' she said, looking jaunty even as she felt the sweet danger of being so alone with him. 'I'd be a bundle of nerves if you weren't.'

He smiled slowly, his teeth a glimmer of white against his firelit face. 'You've got your share of grit – and now we'll make up a couch for the night.'

A couch? There was a dramatic silence. Joanna didn't dare to look at Adam, and she tautened as he came towards her.

'Come,' his fingers touched her shoulder lightly, 'I'll

show you the kind of tree-ferns we collect for a mat-tress.'

'Tree-ferns?' she echoed.

'Yes.' His fingers tightened on her shoulder, as if he knew very well the trend of her thoughts. 'You don't want to sleep on the hard ground, do you? It grows cold in the night and we'll need the rug for a covering.'

'A covering?'

'Little Miss Echo,' he bent his head and his breath stirred teasingly against her cheek, 'keeping warm in the night comes before keeping formal, and I promise not to seduce you . . . if you don't want me to.'

'Oh, really!' She jumped a yard away from him. 'I suppose that's your idea of a joke?'

'You can take it as a joke, if you like.'

She shot him a look, and then he broke into a laugh as he strolled towards the trees. 'Come along, mate. We'll need several armfuls.'

He piled her arms with the feathery, fragrant ferns, and they spread them on the ground near the fire, making several trips until he was satisfied with the softness of this rustic couch beneath the canopy of the raintrees.

Under the greenwood tree, who loves to lie with me . . . ?

Again those words stole through Joanna's mind, provocative as this situation in which she found herself with Adam Corraine. He was making sure the fire was safe within its circle of stones, and Joanna was tensed for the moment when he looked at her, when he said: 'It's time to settle down, Joanna. Take your shoes off. Your feet will feel warmer tucked in the rug.'

With a fast beating heart she removed her sandals and settled down on the mattress of ferns. He had banked it up so there was a head rest, and it was springy, green-scented, and the shock of Adam's touch ran all the way through her as he tucked the ends of the wallaby rug closely around her, the furry side a soft warm tickle.

'D'you feel cosy?' he asked.

'Yes.' Her lashes fluttered like the wings of moths as she gazed up at him and wondered what his thoughts were. For him it wasn't usual to have a girl on his hands, here in the bush, with its mystery and its murmurings.

'You'll sleep fine and be all set for the rest of our trek tomorrow. Feet okay?'

'Warm as toast.' He was so close as he leaned over her to secure the rug beneath the ferns, his shoulders spread wide and strong above her. Her left hand curled against her heart, as if to still its warm, hard beating.

'I'll cat-nap beside the fire,' he said. 'I'm used to it. When we ride out for the big muster, we take turns to keep the billy on the boil so the rangers can have a mug of tea when they feel like it.'

'But you said—' And then she caught the glimmer in his eyes and she realized that he had been teasing her about sharing this ferny bed with her. As if he would – even in the most impersonal way – when at Raintree he had a girl picked out for his future wife; a pretty and demanding young thing, who would want to know how he had spent every minute of this enforced time with Joanna Dowling.

'You said it grew very cold in the night,' she ended.

'I shall sit close to the fire – now don't look worried! I'm an old hand at nodding off without falling into the flames. I'm a stockrider, Joanna. Tough as a well-worn riding-boot.'

'Oh no,' she laughed huskily. 'You're really much kinder than I ever thought—'

'Child,' he quirked a mocking eyebrow, 'don't say nice

things to a man at night. Save them for the daylight – it's much safer.'

'I'm sure you wouldn't lose your head over being called – nice,' she laughed. 'A man likes to be dangerous – like a tiger.'

'Am I dangerous, Joanna?'

'Terribly – but you haven't a fur coat to keep you warm. Won't you take the rug?'

'No.'

'Then you must have your jacket.' She sat up before he could protest and zipped it off. 'Please, Adam – please take it.'

'Does a girl like to be called nice?' he asked.

'Upon occasion.' She snuggled down again into the softness of the rug. Through her lashes she watched him put on the jacket and it gave her a sense of closeness to him that her warmth clung to the material. He zipped it to his throat, and then he stood up and she felt stricken. Never again would she feel so close to him. Never again would it be possible. In the morning they would start early for Raintree ... they had to be home in time for Bonney's party.

'Sleep tight, Joanna,' he said. 'I'll be close by, keeping watch through the night.'

'Good night, Boss.'

He half-turned in the firelight and she saw a smile flicker on his lips. Then he moved out of range, and she lay warm and drowsy in the wallaby rug. She could smell the ferns, the woodsmoke and the forest, and somewhere near the fire there was a low soft whistling ... Adam lulling her to sleep with *Waltzing Matilda*.

The night passed without incident, and Joanna awoke as sunshine shafted through the trees and struck bright across her eyes. She stirred lazily and heard the songbirds in the trees and the lash-like call of a whipbird. A crimson parakeet let out a squawk, as if to rouse her completely from her dreaming. She let the rug slip away from her and she stretched her arms, to which clung tiny pieces of fern. It was in her hair as well, and then she shot to her feet, fully awake, as a large ant crawled across the rug, spidery-legged. She shook the rug vigorously, and then took a look around for Adam. He had set the billy to boil, hung the food satchel on a branch, and left her a note secured by a stone. *Miss D. Have gone foraging for our breakfast. Don't fancy cold turkey – how about you? Mr. C.*

The thought of cold turkey wasn't very appetizing, but as she gazed around at the towering trees, the clumps of ginger against the dense greenery, and the chains of vine that looped themselves about the trunks, she grew nervous in case Adam lost the way back to her. The forest seemed such a vast, impenetrable place to her, and she watched in wonderment as the raintrees unfurled their leaves at the touch of the sun and released the moisture they had collected in the night.

She would go and have a wash while she waited!

When she reached the stream she found blue and green love-birds flying over the water like bright and lovely arrows. And there were clumps of lotus-like flowers floating at the water's edge. The wild beauty of it all was something she would never forget, and she plucked a flower and tucked it into her freshly braided hair. Cooled by her wash, with her pink shirt tucked neatly into her jeans, she made her way back to camp.

As she stepped from among the vines and the clumps of ginger, Adam swung round, grinning at what she had added to his note. *Mr. C. You can't have me for breakfast – I protest. Miss D.*

He glanced at her and his eyes were a clear, startling grey in his beard-shadowed face. They flashed over her, sending a tingle through her.

'I must say you look fresh enough to eat – it's mighty unfair that a man needs a razor before he can look half-way human in the morning.'

He ran a hand over his jaw and smiled ruefully at the rasping sound. He had a strong beard, but then he was a strong man!

'What did you bring back from your hunting trip?' she asked.

'Mangoes. Found a tree loaded with them and brought back a couple for breakfast and a few more to carry with us on our trek. It will grow hot as the sun rises and these fruits are full of juice.'

They made a refreshing breakfast, but all the time Joanna was conscious that this strange idyll with Adam was at the beginning of its end. She looked around, imprinting on her memory the flame flowers, the gaudy little birds that darted upon the cake crumbs she and Adam scattered. One bird was bronze-green, a peacock charmer with a long jewelled tail.

'There's one thing you can say.'

'And what is that?' As she turned her head to look at him she was dappled by a casuarina.

'I made sure you had decent grub even though I was fool enough to forget to refuel the plane. It hasn't been too bad, has it?'

'It's been quite an experience.' She glanced away from him because it was easier to look at the birds than into those quizzical grey eyes. 'I shall remember the rainforest, the wild singing sounds, and billy-boiled tea.'

'Will you remember me, Joanna?'

Her heart thudded and she was even more afraid to

look at him. 'I shall try,' she said lightly. 'You've said one or two memorable things to me.'

'Planning to join your sister quite soon?' He emptied the billy-can over the fire and the smoke spiralled upwards.

'I have almost enough for my fare, but I shall stay of course until you find a replacement for me.'

'I wouldn't want Aunt Charly to be left without any help,' he said a trifle curtly.

'Well, Bonney isn't exactly helpless.' The words were out before she could stop them, and her glance followed them to Adam. He towered there, at the other side of the smoking remnants of the camp fire. His eyes were like steel in his sunburned face.

'Are you suggesting that Bonney could replace you?' he demanded.

'I'm sure it wouldn't do her any harm to help around the house,' Joanna said valiantly. 'She might burn a few steaks – I did myself at the beginning – but it's surely a good thing for a girl to know how to cook and keep house. You said yourself that you like everyone to pull their weight at Raintree, and Bonney isn't a child any more – well, you know that for yourself.'

'No, she isn't a child,' he agreed, 'but you know my reason for spoiling her a little.'

'Yes.' Joanna felt as if a knife turned in her heart. He meant the girl for his wife, so he was justified in making a fuss of her – but what sort of a wife would she make for him if she was spoiled and waited on like a princess? A man like Adam needed a *woman*. Someone who loved him with warmth and passion and a willingness to share the crest of the wave and the troughs. Bonney was as pretty as a picture, but she was also as shallow as one. She was better suited for a man like Vance, who liked to skim the cream off the surface of life.

'We'd better be making a move,' said Adam. 'Time's getting on and we've quite a long walk ahead of us.'

'I'll go and wash the billy and the cups.' She took them and hurried off among the trees to the stream ... there were tears in her eyes and as she knelt to rinse the can and the cups, the flower fell from her hair and floated away on the water.

So began the final lap of their trek through the rain-forest, a riot of vegetation, roots that tripped and clung, insects that buzzed in the humid air. Joanna brushed a weary hand across her eyes, hazy with fatigue and per-spiration, and plodded on in the wake of Adam, who threw encouraging words over his shoulder, who paused now and again to hand her the water-flask.

'Not much further to go,' he shot her a smile and brushed a green fly from her cheek. 'See, the path ahead is filling up with sunlight, which means the trees are thin-ning out. How are your feet? You seem to be stumbling a bit.'

'It's because I'm tired – just a little.'

'Then here goes, now you haven't the strength to fight me.' A steely arm swept around her and lifted her. She murmured a protest, but he pulled her head against his shoulder, so that she felt the vigour and hardness of him, and couldn't have said another word if she had tried.

Gradually the green-gold light shifted from his face, and the undergrowth became less entangled. The dap-pling of sunshine turned to broad, bright shafts and the canopy opened overhead to reveal the vivid blue of the afternoon sky. The leaves of the raintrees shimmered as they caught the sun, the tufted acacias gleamed yellow, and Joanna caught her breath as they came out of the forest and faced a rustic bridge that arched across a gorge that burned with coloured lichens.

'Across the bridge and we're home at last,' he said.

She waited for him to put her down, but he walked to the middle of the bridge before he did so, and it seemed to her a symbolic gesture, as if only so far could the strange intimacy of their adventure be carried.

At the bottom of the gorge a river raced over rocks and a sunlit falls made thunder and spray. The scene was awesome, beautiful, and there were no words to describe Joanna's feelings as she and Adam walked on towards Raintree.

They came to the house from the rear, a pair of tired travellers, hot, thirsting for frosted drinks, cool showers and the comfort of their beds for a few hours.

Someone stood on the veranda ... a voice called their names, and a girlish figure came running across the grass to throw eager young arms about Adam's neck.

CHAPTER NINE

'ADAM . . . darling Adam!' The girl hugged him. 'When you didn't arrive home yesterday, Aunt Charly got in touch with the Brennans and we were told that you left for home in the *morning*. Vance and some of the men are out looking for you both . . .' Bonney ran out of breath and with her arms still chained about his neck she leaned away to search his face. 'You look all right . . . whatever happened?'

'We ran out of fuel and had to make a forced landing.' There was a deep crease in his cheek as he smiled down at Bonney.

The girl shot a look at Joanna and took in swiftly her fair dishevelled hair, and the flying-jacket that hung from her shoulders. 'You mean – it's taken you all this time to reach home?'

'I'm afraid so.' He gave a dry laugh. 'Now let's leave the explanations until later, honey. Joanna is rocking on her feet, and I'm about to die of wanting a long cool beer.'

'I'll run and tell Aunt Charly you're here and safe!'

Bonney sped away, and Joanna felt Adam's gaze upon her. She braved his eyes and saw the little twist of a smile on his lips. 'You mustn't mind if we arouse a bit of curiosity,' he drawled. 'You're an attractive blonde, and one or two people are bound to wonder if I behaved like a gentleman all the time.'

'Those who really know you won't be in any doubt, Adam.' Colour stole into her cheeks, and when they reached the veranda steps she added sincerely, 'I want to thank you for all your patience and consideration towards a greenhorn.'

'I want to thank you, Joanna, for being a girl who smiles at a predicament. If you had been the sort who gets into a flap, I shouldn't have been kind or patient. It's been a pleasure, Miss Dowling, being plane-wrecked with you.'

It was as if he called her darling, and confused, wanting now to be alone, she hastened indoors and along the paved breezeway that ran through the house. The sound of Aunt Charly's stick could be heard, and as she rounded the passage she came face to face with a woman on whom anxiety had left its mark.

'Joanna ... my dear!'

'It's all right.' Joanna hugged her. 'We're both fine.'

'I was so afraid for you both ... and yet, knowing Adam ...' Aunt Charly looked directly into Joanna's eyes, as if she sensed that Joanna had fallen in love with him. 'Poor child, you're whacked out! You must rest. I'll send Peg to coddle you.'

'You're kind.' Joanna was glad to get away to her room, cool, shaded and quiet, and Peg, the young coloured girl, was no intrusion when she came with her soft, good-natured smile to help Joanna freshen up. After her shower it felt good to slip into cotton pyjamas and then into bed. Peg had brought her a jug of fruit juice, and that was all she wanted for now.

'You sleep awhile, Miss Jo, and then you be all nice and ready for the party. Miss Bonney was that worried ... she thought it would be cancelled. Now everything fine again. The Boss is back safe.'

Joanna smiled drowsily. 'Come and wake me, Peg, when it's time to get dressed for the party.'

'I will, Miss Jo.'

The door closed softly and Joanna was alone with her thoughts, which for a while disturbed her and wouldn't let her rest. She closed her eyes and saw again the look Bonney had given her – it had been unmistakably a jealous look, that of a girl who regarded Adam as her private property.

She slept after that, as if her tired mind and body could take no more ... and it was sundown when she awoke, feeling very much refreshed. She was still alone. Peg had not yet returned to tell her it was time to prepare for the party, but the afterglow at the windows beckoned her and she slipped from her bed and went to watch the dying flames in the sky and the way Raintree Valley filled with violet shadows.

Adam's land, so much a part of the man, with unexpected beauty hiding among its rugged planes, and as she gazed from the window she saw a band of horsemen cantering homewards, and the tall rider at the head of them was Vance without a doubt. In the dusk light he resembled Adam, but she felt no tingling thrill, such as she had suppressed on more than one occasion when she had seen the Boss astride his raking chestnut, flashing his eyes over his beloved valley.

As the men rode nearer she heard them laughing and talking, and she guessed that Adam had sent a messenger to bring them back from their searching. There would be no smiles if anything ever happened to the Boss; there would be only a dreadful sense of being cast adrift from a firm and dependable rudder.

'Yippee!' A broad-brimmed hat went flying into the air, and Joanna gave a soft laugh. Yes, they had heard right enough that Adam Corraine was back where he belonged.

She put on the light and was brushing her hair when

Peg poked her head round the door. 'You're up and awake, Miss Jo!' The girl was smiling all over her face as she came into the room, carrying a square box with gold lettering on it. 'You must open this right away, and no arguments.'

Joanna eyed the box with wide-eyed curiosity. 'Who sent it and who said so?'

'A man, Miss Jo.' Peg was giggling.

'A man?' Joanna took a look at the lettering on the box. *Madame Jeanne,* she read. *Costumier and dressmaker.* 'Oh!' Her startled eyes met Peg's. 'Is it for me?'

'For you and no one else, Miss Jo.'

With hands that were a trifle unsteady Joanna lifted the lid and the folds of tissue paper, and her breath caught in her throat. A dress was revealed, of deep blue chiffon, lovely and misty as moonlight on water. There was a card in a little envelope. *Miss D. This is to replace the dress I ruined with the fire extinguisher. Now no British arguments! Mr. C.*

Joanna was speechless. She hadn't dreamed that Adam would be as good as his word and replace the dress she had worn at the barbecue. He was always so busy that she had felt sure he wouldn't give it another thought. 'The dress came with Bonney's presents on the mail plane,' Peg told her. 'The colour matches your eyes, Miss Jo.'

Joanna could feel herself blushing and she told herself not to be foolish. Adam would have asked Aunt Charly's advice about the dress and she would have suggested blue, and given him the measurements which had been taken for the white overalls Joanna wore in the kitchen. Those had been cut out and machined by a woman from the village.

'I won't keep you, Peg,' she said. 'By the way, does

Aunt Charly need my help with the last-minute preparations?'

'No, everything is ready.' Peg hesitated by the door and her smile was rather shy. 'You'll look a real pleasure in that dress, Miss Jo. I bet the Boss hopes you'll wear it for the party.'

'Yes,' Joanna smiled and fondled the blue chiffon. 'We want everything to be just right for Bonney.'

'She's that excited,' Peg laughed. 'You'd think something extra special was in the wind.'

After Peg had gone, Joanna dressed for the party and pondered the girl's parting words. What surprise was in store for everyone tonight? Was Bonney's gift from Adam to take the shape of a diamond ring?

Joanna smoothed the silky-chiffon folds of the lovely dress he had given her. It fitted perfectly and had a softly draped bodice with a sparkle of tiny stars at the waist and the hem. Her hair fell in soft curves to her shoulders and she wore a coral-pink lipstick. As she studied her reflection in the mirror she wondered if Adam would notice her in the dress and feel a little pleased that it suited her so well.

When she arrived downstairs she found the lounge deserted, and the dining-room equally so. The members of the family must still be dressing, and the guests would not start arriving for another half-hour. She wandered about the dining-room, admiring the flower arrangements, the gloss on the fine old furniture and the way it reflected the light of the festive chandeliers. The long family table had been laid with a damask cloth, sparkling silverware and wine glasses, and big red roses from the schoolmaster's garden clustered in bowls among fronds of fern. Each place was set with a tiny name-plate and she leaned forward to study the placings and found that she was to sit between Vance and Adoniah.

Adam's place was at the head of the table, with Aunt Charly at one side of him, and Bonney at the other side.

As Joanna stood admiring the picture which the table made, she heard a slight sound by the door and swung round to confront a tall, handsome figure in a white dinner-jacket, crisp white shirt and narrow dark trousers. He was smiling, one hand lightly at rest in his pocket, and very slowly his blue eyes travelled over Joanna.

'You look beautiful,' he said. 'I'm glad my cousin didn't let you get scratched and bitten and exhausted during your ordeal in the rain-forest. But then Adam knows the place like the palm of his hand, and he's a born knight gallant.'

'Yes.' The smile she gave Vance was a trifle uncertain. 'With Adam it wasn't too much of an ordeal. He found food for us, and water, and I thought the rain-forest rather beautiful. The plane isn't too much damaged—'

'Poor old Bony-bird,' he said, and then he came towards Joanna and before she could retreat he took her by the shoulders and held her gently but firmly. 'Do you remember when we flew among the stars, Joanna? It was very pleasant, wasn't it? We seemed on the edge of something big, and then slowly it was lost like stardust in the sand, and we knew ourselves friends instead of lovers.'

She gazed back at him and saw that his smile was nostalgic, as if no more would he banter about marrying her; as if he realized at last that love was a serious and passionate thing, not just a game.

'I was very anxious about you and Adam,' he went on. And then he broke into his gay smile. 'We didn't want Bonney's party to be spoiled, did we?'

She laughed and relaxed. 'Aunt Charly has made the table look superb. Look at the roses, Vance!'

'Gorgeous, aren't they?' He smiled down at her instead. 'I'd like to kiss you, just to say I'm glad you're alive and well and living here at Raintree.'

She didn't resist because she knew that his kiss would be that of a friend. Then as he bent his head and his lips touched her face, someone else strode into the room, a brown hand arrested at his bow-tie as he came to an abrupt halt just inside the doorway. Over Vance's shoulder Joanna met eyes that seemed to have the sky inside them. Stern and still they looked right at her, and then he swung on his heel.

'Excuse me!' he said pointedly. 'I'll go out and come in again.'

'Adam!' Vance straightened with a laugh and turned to his cousin.

'All I wanted,' Adam had faced round again and his flash of sternness was replaced by his quizzical smile, 'was help with my tie. I'm clumsy tonight – can't seem to get the darn thing to look right.'

'Let me—' Joanna moved towards him, and she was acutely aware of his height and his masculine aliveness as she lifted her hands and fixed his tie for him. She didn't dare to raise her eyes from the narrow bow, black against his white shirt and dinner-jacket. She was more afraid of Adam since she had come to love him. His frown could hurt; his smile could make her knees go weak, and she was terrified of giving herself away to him, or anyone else.

'Thank you.' He spoke formally. 'I'm glad to see that the mail-order dress suits you, Joanna. You look very different tonight from the jungle waif of last night.'

'It was kind of you to buy me the dress.' She had built her defences and was holding them up with a gallant smile. Then aware that Vance was watching the by-play with an inquisitive glint in his eye, she turned towards the door. 'I'll go and see if Aunt Charly wants me for anything.'

As she walked from the room, Vance's voice followed her. 'That is a sweet young woman,' he said. Adam didn't say anything.

The party went with a swing from the moment Adam proposed the birthday toast, to the moment when they rose to go to the room which had been prepared for dancing. Bonney looked as pretty as a bouquet in a mimosa-yellow dress, with a flower tucked into her glossy dark hair. Her eyes shone with excitement as she blew out the candles on her cake and made a wish. She smiled at Adam, and he in turn was looking at her, his lean fingers playing with the stem of his wine glass. His gaze dwelt on the pearls that glowed milkily against the honey of her young throat, and she put up a hand to them, Joanna noticed, and seemed to go shy for a moment.

Someone started the radiogram and couples began to dance. Tye was at Joanna's side, and with a smile she moved into his arms and they circled the floor. Aunt Charly sat talking to Adoniah. In her gold-brown lace, with colour in her cheeks, she looked very handsome, and very happy tonight, as if she too had made a wish that looked like coming true.

'Grand party,' murmured Tye. 'I think everyone is extra gay tonight because we were all so anxious about you and the Boss. How does it feel, Joanna, to be so popular?'

She looked at him with a smile in her eyes, but she felt a little sad at heart. She had grown so fond of the Raintree Valley folks, and they had shown her tonight that she was more than welcome among them. But it couldn't last, not for her. Even as she danced with Tye, pretty Bonney was talking eagerly to Adam.

Someone moved through the dancers to join the couple. It was Vance, and he was laughing in his gay way as he leaned down to Bonney, as if to ask what the conspiracy was about.

'Our party girl sure is pleased with herself,' said Tye. 'Look, Adam is holding up his hand – he wants everyone to stop and listen to him!'

The music died away, and the chattering ceased, and all eyes were fixed expectantly upon Adam as he stepped into the centre of the room, one hand leading Bonney forward. 'I have some very happy news for all of you,' he said smilingly. 'Some of you may already have guessed from the light in Bonney's eyes that she herself is extra happy tonight . . .'

He raised the girl's left hand to his lips, and everyone gasped as they caught sight of the diamond ring sparkling on her engagement finger. Vance stood at one side of Adam, while Aunt Charly leaned forward in her chair, the gleam of happy tears in her eyes.

Joanna wanted Adam to have his happiness, but it was too unbearable for her to watch. Gathering her filmy skirts into her hands she withdrew silently from the room, a blue shadow that skimmed along the breezeway and sped out of a door on to the veranda. She didn't stop running until she reached the rear of the house, where all was quiet but for the night-time chirring that came from the trees. She stood and caught her breath, and fought back her own tears of pain. She wanted Adam of all men to have all he desired, but it hurt . . . much more than she had ever dreamed . . . to see him kiss Bonney's hand and announce the engagement . . .

There were cries of congratulation from inside the

house, then the music started up again, the sound of *Dream Lover*, old and smoochy. Her cold hands clenched the veranda rail, she breathed the poignant scent of clustering flowers, and gazed at the silvery slip of a moon that gemmed the sky. It was a perfect night to have a man whisper his love, but she stood alone and heard only the drift of music and the occasional chirp of a restless bird.

'Joanna?'

A man's voice spoke her name, and as she whirled from the rail the moonlight gleamed on a white dinner-jacket and smooth dark head. She waited tensely ... she was going to find it hard to make light-hearted conversation with Vance ...

'Joanna, why did you leave the party?'

He came nearer, and then another step nearer, and Joanna's wide blue eyes collected into them the image of a strong-boned, serious face, with eyes that held the thrill of lightning.

'Why did you run away?' he demanded.

She backed against the rail, not understanding why he should be here when Bonney was inside the house. 'I – I felt like a breath of air—' she whispered.

'Couldn't be that you couldn't bear to see Vance become engaged to Bonney?'

'What?' She stared at him, unbelievingly. 'Vance ... Bonney?'

'Yes, my girl.' Suddenly he was close to her, her blue chiffon brushing his white jacket. She saw his face clearly, the flash in his eyes, the nerve that flickered beside his mouth. 'Can't take it, never could, the idea that you could love anyone but me!'

'Adam—'

'Yes, Adam!' Now he mocked, now he touched her

arms, now he drew her from the rail and held her so she couldn't get away from him. 'Why did you run away just now? Did you think Bonney was getting engaged to me?'

'Yes—'

'Did you, Joanna?' Now he laughed softly, and she thrilled to the touch of his hand on her fair hair, and was caressed by his eyes, no longer guarded but wide open for her to see what they held.

'Both Aunt Charly and myself had the hope that Vance would come to love Bonney – well, it seems they realized how they felt about each other during the time he had that bad hand. They're well matched, Joanna. A couple should be that way ... and we knew in the rain-forest, didn't we, that all the wild loveliness had a meaning for us. I wanted to put it into words, I wanted to tell you how much you meant to me, but it was too dangerous. I wanted nothing to spoil the moment when I came to you and claimed you for my own.'

'Adam, are you sure?' She searched his face; she had to be utterly certain that this quixotic man was not declaring he loved her because they had spent a day and a night alone in the rain-forest. 'I couldn't bear it if you were just being gallant—'

'Gallant?' With rough tenderness he crushed her close against him. 'I've never wanted anything on this earth as I want you, my girl. I said all along that you wouldn't marry Vance or anyone else. You marry me! And if you care so much about going to New Zealand to see Viviana, then we'll go there for our honeymoon. Would you like that?'

'I'd love it.' And shaken by a delayed storm of joy she buried her face against his shoulder and savoured the feel of his arms, the strength and integrity and exciting maleness of him. 'I love you, Adam. I love you so much. Even when we fought. Even when I believed that you wanted Bonney.'

'Bonney's my ward,' he said tenderly. 'You are my girl. Right from the start, from the moment I made you fight to stay at Raintree. I had to find out if your spirit matched your lovely face, and it did, Joanna. Even in the plane, with the coral reef jagging beneath us, you kept up your spirits, and mine, and I knew if we survived that landing I'd waste no more time about claiming you. I could only hope that you cared for me. I told myself that if you didn't, then I'd make you care.'

She smiled at the very idea of not caring for him, and then she caught her breath as he enfolded her close to his heart and took her lips in a long and loving kiss. It was wonderful, to surrender lips and heart and all her future to Adam Corraine. It was a dream come true . . . his arms and his kisses a thrilling reality.

'A minister will be flying to the valley to marry Bonney and Vance,' he whispered. 'Shall we make it a double wedding?'

'Yes – oh yes!'

'Sweet Joanna.' He kissed her soft hair. 'I have my own word for love, you know. It's cherish. I wish to cherish you all our days together at Raintree Valley.'

'I can think of nothing I'd like more, Adam, than to be cherished by you in this valley of raintrees.'

And then she reached up on her toes and kissed lovingly his lean, warm, sun-weathered cheek. She had come to the valley to stay, and her smile of joy was enclosed in her eyes as Adam held her even closer to him and kissed her as if he would never stop.

FREE!
Harlequin Romance Catalogue

Here is a wonderful opportunity to read many of the Harlequin Romances you may have missed.

The HARLEQUIN ROMANCE CATALOGUE lists hundreds of titles which possibly are no longer available at your local bookseller. To receive your copy, just fill out the coupon below, mail it to us, and we'll rush your catalogue to you!

Following this page you'll find a sampling of a few of the Harlequin Romances listed in the catalogue. Should you wish to order any of these immediately, kindly check the titles desired and mail with coupon.

F   FC 372

Have You Missed Any of These
Harlequin Romances?

All books listed are 50c.   Please use the handy order coupon.

B

Have You Missed Any of These Harlequin Romances?

☐ 1186 SOMEONE ELSE'S HEART Barbara Allen	☐ 1342 THE FEEL OF SILK Joyce Dingwell
☐ 1190 THE SHADOW AND THE SUN Amanda Doyle	☐ 1345 THREE NURSES Louise Ellis
☐ 1192 THE CERTAIN SPRING Nan Asquith	☐ 1346 A HOUSE CALLED KANGAROO Gladys Fullbrook
☐ 1195 SPREAD YOUR WINGS Ruth Clemence	☐ 1347 THE TRUANT SPIRIT Sara Seale
☐ 1199 JOHNNY NEXT DOOR Margaret Malcolm	☐ 1348 REVOLT, AND VIRGINIA Essie Summers
☐ 1202 LAND OF HEART'S DESIRE Catherine Airlie	☐ 1350 ABOVE RUBIES Mary Cummins
☐ 1203 THE LUCKY ONE Marjorie Lewty	☐ 1351 THE GIRL FOR GILLGONG Amanda Doyle
☐ 1205 THE SUN AND THE SEA Marguerite Lees	☐ 1354 WHEN LOVE'S BEGINNING Mary Burchell
☐ 1206 SUBSTITUTE FOR LOVE Henrietta Reid	☐ 1355 RISING STAR Kay Thorpe
☐ 1215 SOFT IS THE MUSIC Jane Beech	☐ 1358 HOME TO WHITE WINGS Jean Dunbar
☐ 1227 A MAN APART Jane Donnelly	☐ 1359 RETURN TO TREMARTH Susan Barrie
☐ 1230 CROWN OF CONTENT Janice Gray	☐ 1360 THIS DESIRABLE RESIDENCE Hilda Nickson
☐ 1232 A DAY LIKE SPRING Jane Fraser	☐ 1362 STRANGER BY MY SIDE Jeannette Welsh
☐ 1233 A LOVE OF HER OWN Hilda Pressley	☐ 1363 STAR DUST Margaret Malcolm
☐ 1234 DESERT GOLD Pamela Kent	☐ 1364 ONE LOVE Jean S. Macleod
☐ 1235 LOVE AS IT FLIES Marguerite Lees	☐ 1366 DESIGN FOR LOVING Margaret Baumann
☐ 1236 JEMIMA Leonora Starr	☐ 1367 INTERLUDE IN ARCADY Margery Hilton
☐ 1237 THE LAST OF THE MALLORY'S Kay Thorpe	☐ 1368 MUSIC I HEARD WITH YOU Elizabeth Hoy
☐ 1239 THIS WISH I HAVE Amanda Doyle	☐ 1370 THE WAYS OF LOVE Catherine Airlie
☐ 1240 THE GREEN RUSHES Catherine Airlie	☐ 1371 DANCING ON MY HEART Belinda Dell
☐ 1246 THE CONSTANT HEART Eleanor Farnes	☐ 1372 ISLE OF POMEGRANATES Iris Danbury
☐ 1247 LAIRD OF STORR Henrietta Reid	☐ 1373 THE PIED TULIP Elizabeth Ashton
☐ 1251 VENICE AFFAIR Joyce Dingwell	☐ 1374 FORTUNE'S LEAD Barbara Perkins
☐ 1253 DREAM COME TRUE Patricia Fenwick	☐ 1375 THE KINDLED FIRE Essie Summers

All books listed are 50c.   Please use the handy order coupon.
C

GOLDEN HARLEQUIN LIBRARY

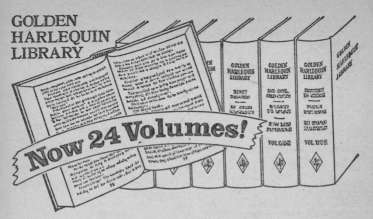

Now 24 Volumes!

Harlequin readers will be delighted! We've collected seventy two of your all-time favourite Harlequin Romance novels to present to you in an attractive new way. It's the Golden Harlequin Library.

Each volume contains three complete, unabridged Harlequin Romance novels, most of which have not been available **since** the original printing. Each volume is exquisitely bound in a fine quality rich gold hardcover with royal blue imprint. And each volume is priced at an unbelievable $1.75. That's right! Handsome, hardcover library editions at the price of paperbacks!

This very special collection of 24 volumes (there'll be more!) of classic Harlequin Romances would be a distinctive addition to your library. And imagine what a delightful gift they'd make for any Harlequin reader!

Start your collection now. See reverse of this page for full details.